PRAISE FOR JAMES MELVILLE AND *THE RELUCTANT RONIN*

"Highly recommended for mystery readers of refined taste."

Chicago Sun-Times

"Melville's Otani novels could be described by the Japanese adjective *shibui* . . . elegant, restrained and in the best possible taste."

Los Angeles Times

"Fascinating layers of Japanese customs and manners unpeeled as Otani investigates politely. Superior mix of crime and culture."

The London *Times*

"Melville captures [Japan] as it is today with the oriental precision of an expert calligrapher. . . . Otani is one of the most expertly drawn figures in modern detective fiction who deserves a wider audience, not just because he is authentic but because he and his world are so original."

Punch

Also by James Melville
Published by Fawcett Books:

Superintendent Otani Mysteries

WAGES OF ZEN

A SORT OF SAMURAI

THE CHRYSANTHEMUM CHAIN

THE NINTH NETSUKE

DEATH OF A DAIMYO

SAYONARA, SWEET AMARYLIS

THE DEATH CEREMONY

GO GENTLY, GAIJIN

KIMONO FOR A CORPSE

Other Fiction

THE IMPERIAL WAY

THE RELUCTANT RONIN

James Melville

FAWCETT CREST • NEW YORK

*For Thomas and Sheila Singleton,
in gratitude and affection*

AUTHOR'S NOTE

Hyogo is a real prefecture whose police force is based in Kobe. Kansai Television is the leading regional commercial channel, and Osaka Women's University is a distinguished private foundation. It is important therefore for me to stress that all the characters in this story are as fictitious as Dejima Pharmaceutical Company.

和蘭陀美人殺人事件

Prelude

To: Superintendent OTANI, Tetsuo, Commanding Hyogo Prefectural Police Force

From: Superintendent-General, National Police Agency

DEATH OF A FOREIGN NATIONAL

You are hereby informed that I have ordered an internal inquiry into the conduct of the investigation of the death of Netherlands citizen MARIANNA VAN WIJK by you and by Inspectors NOGUCHI Hachiro, KIMURA Jiro and HARA Takeshi, all serving under your command.

The inquiry will be carried out by Senior Superintendent NITTA Eiji of the Criminal Investigation Department of this Agency, to whom you will without delay submit your full report on the case and thereafter make yourself and the other named officers available for questioning as and when he requires.

Senior Superintendent Nitta's findings will be laid before me in due course, after which I shall decide whether or not disciplinary action should be taken in accordance with the procedures laid down in Agency Regulations and Service Instructions.

The document bore both the official and the personal seals of the Superintendent-General, and Otani pushed it to one side before opening the envelope marked 'STRICTLY PERSONAL' which had also arrived from Tokyo that day. It contained a handwritten, friendly note from Senior Superintendent Nitta.

> Otani-san: A note in haste to reassure you. For reasons which I will explain when we meet the S-G had no alternative but to set up a formal internal inquiry. You'll obviously have to warn the other three that I shall want to talk to them, but all's reasonably well that ended well, so tell them not to lose too much sleep. Kinoshita and your other old friends here send their regards. Nitta

Otani took a deep breath and reached again for the print-out of the report he had drafted on the basis of Hara's meticulously ordered account, Kimura's extensive notes and several conversations with Noguchi, and which his clerk had put on to the word-processor. It was his own contribution that he had to be particularly careful about, editing it in such a way that it might stand up not only to the suspicious scrutiny of the district prosecutor but also to highly professional analysis by Nitta and his team at the NPA. He had known Nitta of the rubbery comedian's face and bluff, deceptive kindliness of manner too long to be in any doubt about either the quality of his mind or the subtlety of his skills both as an investigator and as an office politician. The reassuring covering note did nothing to weaken Otani's conviction that Nitta would give him a rough ride.

Outside his open office window the heavy traffic of the Kobe port area rumbled unceasingly. Inside the big, shabby old room the only sound was the whirring of the bright blue plastic blades of the electric fan on its tall stand swinging automatically to and fro through an arc, rustling the papers

2

on Otani's desk each time the tepid breeze it generated reached them. For Otani himself had read no more than the opening paragraphs before falling into a reverie, reflecting that his own part in the affair had begun long before the events in which the National Police Agency were so interested.

Chapter 1

"**T**WELVE *THOUSAND*?" HANAE OTANI REPEATED weakly, and her daughter Akiko nodded in confirmation.

"On a single plant grown in a space of ten square metres. And nearly all beauties. And when you think what you have to pay for tomatoes even in the market, or the food basement of a cheap and nasty store like this . . ." She dismissed their surroundings with a contemptuous gesture. "Akira saw it when he had to take one of his English business contacts to the Science Expo at Tsukuba last month. Or one just like it, rather. Apparently the Emperor had been very struck by it during a visit only about three weeks earlier and the plant had produced another six hundred fruit by the time Akira got there."

Hanae tried hard to conceal the concern she felt as she smiled encouragingly at Akiko and at the same time kept a watchful eye on four-year-old Kazuo Shimizu. Her grandson was perched happily in the open cockpit of an All Nippon Airways jumbo jet studying the flashing lights of the instrument panel as the toy lurched and swayed through the brief surge of activity which had cost her yet another hundred yen. Akiko's low opinion of the department store on the featureless northern outskirts of Osaka was fair enough. It was on

4

the seedy side. Its layout was conventional, but the handbags and costume jewellery on the ground floor were tawdry, the men's shirts which had briefly caught her eye on the second floor were cheap imports from Korea, and the uniformed girl who operated the lift up to the Children's Paradise and Garden Centre on the roof was both spotty and pudgy; a far cry from her svelte sisters at the prestigious Hanshin or Hankyu stores Hanae usually patronised in Osaka's downtown Umeda shopping centre or in central Kobe, which were in any case easier to get to from her home in the dormitory suburb of Rokko between the two cities.

On the other hand this down-market *depaato* was conveniently close to Kazuo's exclusive kindergarten, and he was deeply attached to the mechanical and electronic wonders of its Children's Paradise. Hanae had fallen into the habit of popping over once or twice a month to wait with Akiko outside the kindergarten gate until the little boy emerged to show off his latest feats of drawing or writing and be rewarded with a treat of some kind, and since her daughter strictly forbade bean-jam buns and other gooey edibles a few goes on the space capsules, bullet trains or police motorbikes were the obvious answer.

Since the Shimizus' return from Akira's assignment to the London office of the trading company for which he worked, Kazuo had been a delight to his grandparents. It was comical that he still came out with English words and phrases from time to time, but reassuring that within a few weeks he was parroting slogans from television commercials and chattering happily in Japanese. The principal of the kindergarten had initially taken a gloomy view of the probable extent of the child's alienation from the Japanese way of life and made all manner of difficulties about accepting him, and Hanae suspected that although nothing had been said, his grandfather might have pulled a few strings to secure Kazuo's eventual admission. One simply had to be ruthless in the matter of education—all being well their grandson would now pass more or less automatically into the primary, junior and senior high schools run by the same respected private foundation and have every prospect of entrance to a top university in due course. And needless to say early reports from Kazuo's teacher Miss Kimata suggested that he scarcely noticed the differences in his new environment and would have no problems of adjustment.

Hanae wished ardently that she could feel as confident about her daughter, who was looking altogether more washed out and discontented than she should have done as the thirty-four-year-old wife of the newly promoted director of an important department of a major trading company with who knew what even dizzier prospects before him. Settling into the neat, heavily mortgaged little house in Senri New Town must of course have been quite a business, but surely not without its excitements, and Hanae had expected to be hearing more about the parent-teacher association and the neighbourhood wives' club than a lot of vague, distracted talk about monster tomato plants.

"No, he's had quite enough for today, Mother," Akiko said as Hanae began to fumble for her purse again. "Do you realise you could probably fly in the real thing for less than that contraption costs per minute? Not that anyone in her right mind living practically under the flight path to Osaka Airport would want to."

"Your father says that when they open the new international airport in the bay we shall probably have a much noisier time than you do now in Senri," Hanae pointed out as Akiko decisively scooped the little boy out of his technological nest and helped him hoist on to his back the huge regulation satchel from which he would rarely allow himself to be parted.

Forty-five minutes later Hanae sat alone and thoughtful in the back of a taxi inching its way into the heart of Osaka. This was an absurd extravagance. She could have gone by subway train in an eighth of the time for a sixth of the price, but it seemed worth paying for the solitude. Besides, only the other day her husband had pointed out that even if they went almost everywhere by taxi they would still spend less than it would cost them to own, maintain and garage a car, let alone actually drive anywhere in it. Moreover, the taxi was air-conditioned, and Hanae needed a respite from the

6

summer heat to assimilate properly what Akiko had told her over a quick lunch, in hurried half-sentences while keeping an eye on Kazuo as he steadily demolished the highly coloured contents of his Kiddy Platter. There was a miniature Japanese flag made of paper attached to a toothpick stuck into the hamburger, and he insisted on having it fixed to the straw hat which formed part of the summer uniform of his kindergarten. Hanae had done it for him, while she listened carefully and incredulously to her daughter.

So there was after all some point to all the babbling about the monster tomato plant, grown by a hydroponic method christened "hyponica culture" by its elderly inventor, who had, it seemed, devoted himself to it late in life after making a fortune in the plastics business. Sitting in the taxi, Hanae belatedly remembered reading about it somewhere, and recalled thinking at the time that the emphasis on circulating a vigorously aerated nutrient solution round the roots of plants made it sound rather like keeping tropical fish.

At all events Akira Shimizu was apparently persuaded that it made all the difference in terms of results and cost-effectiveness in comparison with the conventional hydroponic farming which had already caught on in many parts of land-hungry Japan, and the long and short of it was that he was determined to raise enough money to give up his job and become a high-technology market gardener.

Hanae had held her tongue with difficulty. The crowded, noisy restaurant was no place for a serious conversation, and in any case such matters were not for discussion in Kazuo's hearing. Far better that mother and daughter should have a quiet talk one morning soon during kindergarten hours—at least there was a crumb of comfort in the thought that Akiko uncharacteristically seemed to want to discuss it at all. Hanae often reminded herself and her husband that they were exceptionally fortunate to be in such close contact with the Shimizus as they were. In normal circumstances, as a Japanese daughter of Japanese parents, Akiko on marriage would have been to all intents and purposes lost to them, and any children she bore almost exclusively the concern of the Shimizu family.

Akira Shimizu had been brought up unconventionally, though. When first meeting his architect father Hanae had been struck by his corduroy jacket and beautiful orange woollen necktie, and been in some danger of falling a little in love with Akiko's future mother-in-law, a theatrical designer of some repute with a creatively irresponsible attitude to housekeeping which both shocked and delighted Hanae.

By that time of course the student unrest of the late sixties had simmered down, Akira had repudiated or been repudiated by the Maoist splinter group of the All-Japan Student Federation he had led at Kobe University, and like a surprising number of other energetic and effective firebrands had been recruited into the ranks of big business by an imaginative talent-spotter. Hanae had been mystified to infer that Akira's apparently untraumatic enrolment in the service of capitalism had been observed by his parents with mingled amusement and disappointment; and this at a time when the Otanis had been only too delighted to notice that the Che Guevara poster had come down from the wall of their daughter's room to be replaced by one of Herbert von Karajan. There were other cheering indications of ideological reconciliation as Akiko's former passionate comradeship with her political mentor was quickly transformed into what looked uncommonly like commitment of a different kind: cheering to her parents, at any rate.

The conservative Otanis and the bohemian Shimizus had taken to each other from the start and it was clear that there would in any case be nothing distant or inhibited about the relationship between the two families; but within two years and before Kazuo's birth came tragedy. An important commission to design a university library in the United States entailed a number of visits there for Akira's father, and his parents were travelling together to be present at the formal opening ceremony of the brilliantly imaginative, critically acclaimed building when their plane crashed into a mountainside and they were both killed. Since then it had been as though Akira had become a son to the Otanis, and Hanae sometimes smiled to herself at the sight of the former militant radical and Superintendent Otani of the Hyogo prefectural

8

police force amicably discussing a few flasks of *sake*. She knew that her husband not only liked but also respected the younger man who had in the old days confronted him so often, and that he was by no means above seeking Akira's advice when he wanted a detached but incisive opinion about some knotty official problem.

Hanae herself was proud of her son-in-law's obvious success in his work, and honest enough to doubt whether Akiko would have become half so lively, tolerant and generous without Akira at her side. The similarity between their given names had become something of a quiet family joke, with Akiko insisting that their respective *karma* were clearly bound up together.

The impression remaining with Hanae after the brief and frustrating conversation in the restaurant was that Akiko was doing her best to convince herself of the rationality of a wild scheme which offered only the vaguest prospects of success in the long term to balance the certainty of immediate anxiety and upheaval. It was all very well for an elderly millionaire to devote himself to producing improbably productive tomato plants; but a very different matter for a family man in his late thirties to abandon a secure and increasingly well-paid job on the strength of a sudden enthusiasm.

Hanae sighed as the taxi crept forward in the company of the dozens of other vehicles negotiating the jammed approaches to the Umeda national and private railway stations and shopping centre, and then became impatient. As they neared the fume-laden gloom of the railway bridge she leant forward and asked the white-gloved driver to let her out by the New Hankyu Hotel instead of negotiating the last two or three hundred metres to the Hanshin Department Store she had originally specified. The hotel entrance was just ahead to their left, but even so it was fully two minutes before the driver managed to edge through the traffic into the left-hand lane. The sidewalks were as busy as the road, with an unceasing flow of pedestrians making their purposeful way to and from the stations, unconsciously and unseeingly skirting the much smaller number of people cutting across the currents, pausing to light a cigarette or even to concentrate on a discussion with a companion.

It was an unremarkable scene, and Hanae was in any case preoccupied with her anxieties; but the golden hair of a tall foreign woman standing to one side of the main throng some fifty metres ahead to the left was so striking that it caught her eye. When she was younger Hanae had deeply envied Western women, and thought how lucky so many of them were to have straight legs and hair of such silky fineness compared with that of oriental women. The fact that in addition that hair might be any of a hundred shades from palest ash-blonde through a whole spectrum of reds and chestnuts to a glossy dark brown, and that if its owner was dissatisfied with the effect it could be dyed most effectively made matters worse.

Japanese hair was black, and that was that. It could be kept that way with the aid of dye and frequently was, by vain people of both sexes battling the advancing years. Otherwise, dyeing was not for respectable women like Hanae but for whores and hostesses in tawdry bars, and she had seen some of the weird and wonderful shades of orange they achieved. In any case Hanae's own hair was greying in a way she neither resented nor attempted to conceal, any more than her husband had when it happened to him a decade previously, and he stoutly maintained that he found her touches of "romance grey" just as attractive as young women claimed to do in the case of men of a certain age.

The foreign woman was, Hanae judged, in her late twenties, and obviously in no way defensive about her stature. She was a least six or seven centimetres taller than the man to whom she was talking with great animation, but her shoes were very far from being flat-heeled, and the froth of hair which glowed like a halo in the sun was certainly not styled so as to minimise her height. Hanae liked the foreigner's cool-looking pale green dress and air of unforced vivacity, and found herself smiling with tolerant understanding when the conversation apparently came to an end and the woman hesitated very briefly and then flung her arms round her companion's neck and kissed him warmly as he embraced her in response. The pair of them seemed oblivious to the glances

10

of mingled amusement and embarrassment their action attracted from passers-by near enough to see what was happening. Hanae's taxi was still some distance away from them when after several seconds the couple separated, the woman joining the stream of people headed for the national railway station.

Hanae was, however, quite near enough to the man when he turned to face for the first time in her direction to recognise him as her son-in-law Akira Shimizu; and to feel as though a cold hand were fumbling at her heart when she saw the expression on his face.

Nobody paid particular attention to Shimizu as he made his way into the elegant tower of glass and steel which housed the main offices of his company. It was near Yodoyabashi, in cheeky proximity to the much larger headquarters of the mighty Sumitomo concern, whose top executives affected to regard the activities of their upstart neighbour as constituting no more than fringe competition. Even so, Shimizu had both in London and since his return to Japan been approached by Sumitomo emissaries on neutral territory with the subtlest of suggestions that he might find more scope for his talents by working for them rather than an increasingly successful business rival.

Within seconds his overheated body responded to the cool, dry air inside the building, and he passed a finger round the inside of his shirt collar to free his neck from its clammy embrace as he waited by the bank of lifts. A young woman, a stranger to him but obviously an employee, came and waited with him. She drew back deferentially when the lift arrived to let him in first, and shyly asked for the seventh floor when he reached out to the button panel and raised an eyebrow at her interrogatively. Shimizu's own office was on the tenth, and it wasn't until the girl passed him on the way out that he noticed the twitch of a smile at the corner of her mouth. Even then it took a second or two for him to take in the knowing, sexually aware quality of her expression, reach hurriedly for a pocket tissue and scrub at his mouth with it.

The amount of lipstick on it when he was finished more

11

than accounted for the look on the girl's face, and Shimizu checked his appearance in the men's room on the tenth floor before walking through the big open-plan office which housed the staff of his department and making for his own desk in the corner. One of the section heads responsible to him half-rose in his seat as he approached and seemed about to intercept him with a query, but Shimizu ignored him as he passed, acknowledging only his secretary who had been on watch for him and waited by his desk with a sheaf of message slips.

He took off his jacket and hung it on a hook on the wall, took the slips of paper from her and leafed through them, then rearranged them in order of priority. A few telephone calls to be returned: nothing of particular importance. Then Shimizu looked up, realising that Miss Shiromoto was still standing there. He forced a smile of the kind which had once come so easily. "Is there something else, Miss Shiromoto?"

She nodded. "I didn't write it down, but a Mr Makoto Aoki rang, wanting to speak to you. Twice. He . . . he wasn't very polite."

Shimizu closed his eyes for half a second and then replied quite calmly. "I'm very sorry to hear that. Please accept my apologies on his behalf." He felt light-headed, as though the blood had drained from his head, and looked down at his hands on the blotter in front of him as though they belonged to somebody else. "Did Mr Aoki leave any message for me?"

Miss Shiromoto spoke very politely, so that Shimizu could scarcely make out the words over the controlled hubbub of the big office. "He just said that he expected to hear from you before the end of the afternoon, and that you knew where to find him."

"I see. Yes, I know his phone number. Thank you. And I'm sorry again that his manner upset you. Aoki can be a disagreeable man."

Shimizu looked at the message slips again and returned two of the routine business calls, hoping afterwards that he had made some kind of sense. At least by then Miss Shiromoto had returned to her own desk and stopped staring at him, whatever she might be thinking. Then he stood up and reached towards his jacket on the wall behind him and turned the pages of the small diary he took from one of the inside pockets as he sank back into his chair. He found the number he needed and began to tap it out, but faltered and replaced the telephone receiver before finishing.

He needed more time to steel himself to respond to Makoto Aoki's command.

Chapter 2

"COMPLETE WRITE-OFF, HE SAID," NOGUCHI GROWLED again as Otani's personal driver edged the car round a particularly acute corner and then had to stop altogether while a uniformed policeman peered suspiciously at them before grudgingly shoving the temporary barrier aside and waving them through. Superintendent Tetsuo Otani was not offended by the patrolman's hesitation. His black and white Toyota Police Special was of course impeccably official, but its occupants did, he realised, present an unorthodox image.

This was because they had just come from the handsomely appointed sports complex which was the principal legacy of the Universiade staged in the city of Kobe a couple of years previously, and more particularly from the Olympic pool where they had been dutifully cheering on the Hyogo prefectural police force's best swimmers, competing in the Kansai regional police sports championships. So they were dressed appropriately; even the driver Tomita. Over the years Otani had seen Tomita out of uniform only rarely, but often enough to have been unsurprised when he turned up at the house to pick him up earlier that Sunday wearing a bright yellow sports shirt and trousers of an unfortunate electric-blue with green plastic shoes.

14

"Yes, Ninja. I heard you the first time," Otani said a little sharply. "I'm still not quite sure why I'm needed so particularly, though." Inspector "Ninja" Noguchi was by comparison with Tomita quite restful to the eye. Otani could not remember how many summers ago it had been since he had first seen the capacious linen jacket his old friend and most trusted colleague was wearing over a surprisingly clean brown open-necked shirt, but it certainly looked very familiar.

He was himself quite nattily got up in a new silver-grey lightweight suit which Hanae had persuaded him to buy against his better judgment. He thought it made him look like a television game show host, especially with the pale blue shirt she had quietly insisted on, but in the event it had seemed right for the informality of the occasion. It would never have done for the commander of the Hyogo force to have shown up in support of his men looking if he was off for a round of golf afterwards, while uniform or one of his four almost identical dark "salaryman" suits would have been equally inappropriate.

"Hara knows what he's doing," Noguchi said equably, seemingly oblivious to the chill in the atmosphere between them as Otani wound his window down and peered out crossly at the burnt-out building now in plain view to their left, coughing as the acrid smell caught at his throat. "Takes a good man to know when to ask advice. Bit different from Kimura. There he is, talking to that fireman."

Tomita brought the car to a halt and leapt out to open the rear door, and by the time Otani had clambered out Inspector Takeshi Hara of the criminal investigation section had approached and saluted respectfully. In spite of his height and substantial bulk Hara was a diffident man with a permanently preoccupied air about him. He was still in his late twenties, one of the new breed of graduate fast-stream entrants. Otani had been dubious about the prospects of his fitting into the headquarters team on transfer from Nagasaki, but to his astonishment Hara and Noguchi had got along famously from the start. Kimura had been predictably prickly with the new man at first, but after some months even he seemed to have achieved an amicable *modus vivendi* with him, leaving Otani

15

to wonder if he was the only one who still found Hara tediously pedantic.

"I must apologise, sir, for having disturbed you this afternoon. I should not have ventured to do so—"

"Yes, yes. Well, never mind, I'm here now. It's not as if our team were doing all that well, anyway. Though I don't see why you had to be so mysterious with Inspector Noguchi on the phone, Hara. Or why you're prowling about here yourself, if it comes to that."

Otani was being deliberately obtuse. He knew perfectly well that in dealing with any and every outbreak the fire brigade would expect and receive police back-up as necessary, usually in the way of traffic and crowd control. He was also well aware of the much more important fact that the senior fire officer on the scene would not have asked for the presence of criminal investigation staff unless he had reason to believe that the circumstances were suspicious.

"If I might be permitted to make my report, sir? I should not have requested your personal presence unless . . ." As Hara hesitated Otani became aware of Noguchi bristling at his side and realised that he was being unreasonable.

"Yes, of course. I'm sorry, Inspector. Start from the beginning, by all means."

"Sir. As headquarters duty officer Assistant Inspector Endo was informed by East Central Division at 11.37 today that the fire brigade was attending a major incident at a four-storey office building in this district, and at 12.23 was further notified that the blaze was being brought under control and that there was no longer any significant threat to neighbouring structures. No further information was received until 14.09, when Mr Endo received a request from East Central Division for specialist support from staff of the headquarters criminal investigation section. Being aware that I was on the premises Mr Endo consulted me, and I at once telephoned East Central myself—"

"The usual suspected arson drill, in other words," Otani cut in, gazing at the smouldering shell of the building. "Saturdays and Sundays are favourite days. Silly really, when you think about it. People are bound to start asking questions. . . ." He was quite ready to expand on the subject but paused when he saw the look in Hara's face. "Sorry again, Hara. Carry on. What is—or was—this place, anyway?"

Hara blinked several times in the face of Otani's demand that he should come to the point, but otherwise disregarded it and ploughed ahead in his own way, often to the back of his superior's head as Otani sized up the physical situation. They were in a comparatively recently redeveloped district well to the east of the Sannomiya rail and bus terminals and shopping complex. Otani passed near the area most days when being driven from his house to the office and back, but couldn't remember actually being there for years, if ever. Before being levelled by wartime bombing it must have been self-contained, a typical warren of flimsy houses, workshops and little places of business serving people who lived and worked in the neighbourhood and probably left it only rarely.

The price of land being what it was the streets were still narrow, but Otani doubted whether many of the families who once lived there were still represented. A few, perhaps. People whose grandfathers had in the hungry post-war chaos been that crucial bit better off, smarter or more entrepreneurial than most and who had developed and redeveloped their own tiny parcels of real estate to the point where three- and four-storey concrete buildings were nowadays the norm. Even the most traditional businesses like rice and sake dealers or sushi and noodle restaurants were now housed on the ground floors of little blocks of apartments or offices.

The bigger league of professional developers had also left their much more conspicuous mark, though, and a good many of the buildings Otani had passed on his way to the scene of the fire and in some cases could still see occupied much larger sites which must in former times have accommodated dozens of families who had seen no alternative to selling out. The neighbourhood now boasted a training school for beauticians, a substantial private maternity hospital and a number of office blocks. The major banks were represented, and the street level of the building immediately opposite formed the premises of a travel agency.

". . . to judge from the name-plates at the entrance are several related enterprises, sir."

Otani wheeled round and stared again directly at Hara. "Yes. I have been listening, Inspector," he said briskly. "Though I'm sure all that will in any case appear in your written report. I'll have a look for myself. Hinomaru Building, eh? Suggest anything to you, Ninja?"

Without waiting for a reply he strode over to the ruined entrance and studied the blackened, barely legible aluminium panel attached to the wall just inside. It took him only a second or two to reinforce his preliminary conclusion, but rather longer to consider how to react to his two colleagues. When he did turn away and look at them his expression was cold and unfriendly.

"It would have been helpful if you had told Inspector Noguchi on the phone that it was *yakuza* premises that had burned down, Hara," he said. "Or are you seriously expecting me to believe that East Central Division didn't think to mention the fact when reporting to our duty officer? All right, I know the national flag of this country isn't the exclusive property of the gangs, and that the word 'Hinomaru' is tacked on to the names of some perfectly respectable consumer goods. But good heavens, man, even the most naive patrolman recruit could hardly fail to put two and two together after a glance at this name-plate! 'Hinomaru Construction Company', 'Hinomaru Leisure Enterprises', 'Hinomaru Loan Company', 'Hinomaru Catering Supplies' . . . the only thing they seem to have left out is 'Hinomaru Pimps and Porno Agency', but that presumably comes under leisure enterprises anyway."

Otani was so busy berating Hara that he didn't notice the look on Noguchi's face, and irritatedly tried to shake off the hand on his forearm. Then strong fingers closed in an unmistakable message and he paused.

"There's a problem," Noguchi said calmly. "Needed you here so as to explain properly. East Central know all about this place, needless to say. So do I. And Hara was told."

"I see. But nobody thought it worth informing me of the fact. I suppose I should be flattered by your confidence that

I would guess for myself.'' Otani turned to glare directly at Noguchi, who released his grip and shuffled in what might have been embarrassment before continuing.

"Could have mentioned it on the way, but Hara thought you ought to see for yourself. Didn't want to put ideas in your head.''

Otani took a deep breath. "Thank you both for your consideration,'' he said carefully. "Now will you please come to the point, Hara, and show me and Inspector Noguchi whatever it is you think I ought to see? When a gang headquarters building burns down we are entitled to doubt from the first any suggestion that it was an act of God. Did they organise it themselves as an insurance swindle, or was it arranged by a rival group? Well, are we going inside, or not?''

Hara hesitantly barred the way. "Not necessary or desirable, sir. I am advised that the structure is in a dangerous condition. The fire brigade's own specialists are inside with two of mine, and we shall be given a technical report in due course. First indications suggest some sort of insurance fraud, in that *yakuza* premises are of course normally never left unattended.''

Otani cocked his head on one side and looked up at the pale moon face in some surprise. "No casualties, then? I could have sworn I heard an ambulance as we were approaching.''

"No *yakuza* casualties, sir. The body of a woman was however found in the remains of a first-floor room, immediately above the one in which the fire is provisionally thought to have originated. She was so dreadfully . . . that is to say, identification might have proved to be extremely difficult—''

"Might have? But didn't?''

"The body is that of an unusually tall woman, sir. Tall even for a Westerner, which the medical examiner at once judged her to have been. His opinion is supported by the contents of the handbag found under the body, which had partially protected it from the flames. These make it reasonable to presume that the victim was Dutch, resident in Tokyo, thirty-two years old and named Marianna van Wijk. The bag

19

contained an Alien Registration Card including that information, as well as certain other items of European origin.''

Otani rubbed his chin. "I see. Nasty business." Then he shook his head. "At least, I don't see, really. What on earth could she have been doing in a building carefully vacated by its owners so that they could set fire to it? Well, it's certainly puzzling, and I shall be very interested to know what emerges when it's looked into properly. All the same, I'm still not clear why you thought it necessary to drag me here in such a hurry, Hara. Why didn't you get hold of Kimura? Foreigners are his job."

"Name doesn't ring a bell with you, then?"

"Name, Ninja? This poor Dutchwoman's name? Of course not. Why on earth should it?" Otani looked from one to the other of his two colleagues in mounting bewilderment. Both were gazing at him intently. "What *is* the matter with you two? It's like trying to get juice from a dried persimmon to find out what you're getting at."

"You could be wrong, Hara," Noguchi growled after an awkward pause. "Where is it? Got it on you?"

Hara nodded and fumbled with the button of the right-hand breast pocket of his tunic, then took from it a transparent self-sealing plastic envelope. Noguchi seized it unceremoniously, turned it over, squinted at it briefly and then held it out in silence to Otani.

It was a scorched but otherwise intact colour photograph taken in the funfair section of the public park on the man-made Port Island in Kobe harbour. A good-looking married couple were swinging their grinning young son by the arms as the older man and woman with them looked on fondly at what could only be their grandson. None of the people in the picture seemed to be aware of the camera, and to judge from the unusual angle Otani guessed the little family group had very probably been snapped from one of the gondolas of the popular Space Ride. He remembered the occasion some seven or eight weeks earlier perfectly well, and had not been conscious that anything was amiss. The photograph was intriguing, though. In it neither his daughter Akiko nor her husband looked anything like as happy as Hanae and he did, and the contrast between them and the joyful little boy was even more marked.

"No mistake, is there?" Noguchi said heavily. "You see the problem now."

Chapter 3

AND WHAT IS THE BIGGEST GROWTH SECTOR IN CRIME according to the National Police Agency annual statistical report? White-collar and computer villainy, that's what. While here we are still in the Stone Age. Hardly started on our own computerisation programme, and having to sit like dummies in the middle of a complex investigation waiting for documents to be sent through the *post* from Tokyo! Good grief, every miserable little commercial enterprise in Japan has electronic mailbox and fax transmission facilities these days. When I think how I've begged and pleaded with the Chief . . ."

Words finally failed Inspector Jiro Kimura and he flung himself back in his chair and sighed theatrically as he reached for a tissue from the box on his desk and dabbed at his forehead. It was hot and stuffy in his cramped little office, and the electric fan perched on top of the filing cabinet stirred the soupy air without really helping much.

"Special delivery is still very fast and efficient," Hara pointed out from the single visitor's seat. "The full details will be here tomorrow, and they were able to give you the essential basic information over the phone, after all. No doubt the Ministry of Foreign Affairs are having to proceed carefully in any case, with the Netherlands Embassy and the Delegation of the European Commission both involved.''

Kimura eyed his colleague warily. For years he had enjoyed his effective monopoly of headquarters expertise in the mysteries of the relationship between foreigners in Japan whether resident or just visiting, the diplomatic and consular authorities charged with their protection when necessary, and the various law-enforcement, fiscal and other agencies which might have an interest in them. It went without saying that police involvement generally implied trouble of some kind, but Kimura liked to think that there was more to it than that, and that the discreet eye he kept on the resident foreign community was evidence of no more than his generalised goodwill towards them and consequent desire to contribute where possible to their well-being. He was fond of pointing out that unlike the vast majority of Japanese who when approached by public opinion pollsters regularly said they wanted nothing to do with foreigners, he liked them. Especially, as Otani commented sourly when the subject came up, if they were European or American, female and aged somewhere between eighteen and sixty.

The son of a diplomat, Kimura had spent some of his formative years in America. His English was fluent and idiomatic, his French serviceable, and he was ideally qualified for his job. There were foreigners and foreigners, of course, and Kimura was perfectly happy to leave the long-established Korean and Chinese communities in Kobe to Ninja Noguchi, but otherwise he revelled in his familiarity with the fine print of the regulations governing the status of *gaijin* in Japan and was at his most efficient when threading his way happily through the formalities involved when one died. Whereas Otani invariably waved away his offers of explanations and gladly left such tiresome manoeuvres to him, the intellectual Hara was proving to be altogether too quick on the uptake and Kimura frowned, his proprietorial instincts offended.

''Ah, yes. Of course. I wouldn't bother yourself too much with that side of things if I were you, though. You've got quite enough on your plate sorting out exactly how and why that fire was started.''

"Very true, Inspector. It has been established, by the way, that we are definitely dealing with a case of arson, presumably by an agent or agents of the building's owners. If this proves to be the case, Penal Code Article 109 would normally apply, with a maximum penalty of seven years' imprisonment since there was no damage to nearby property. The tragic death of the young woman—even if it turns out to have been accidental—does however significantly increase the gravity of the offence, bringing it within the scope of Article 108.''

"If you say so, Hara. And what's so special about Article 108?''

Hara took off his glasses and polished them vigorously. "Setting fire to and burning a building in which persons are actually present can be a capital offence.''

Kimura raised an eyebrow. He had not known this and wondered whether the arsonists had. "Like murder. That's quite interesting, Hara. I've been sitting here wondering what she was doing in the place anyway and rather assuming that although it's hard to conceive of her having any business there she was overcome by fumes and trapped by accident. But supposing she was the *reason* for the fire? Murder dressed up as accidental death, arranged by somebody who didn't know much about the arson laws?''

Hara visibly pondered the hypothesis. "It's difficult to credit,'' he said at last, "but not inconceivable, I suppose. Such an unlikely person to be a murder victim, though; still less to have had connections with organised crime.'' He peered again at the single photocopied sheet of paper Kimura had passed to him at the beginning of their conversation. "I had never heard of such a thing as a European Business Study Fellow before.''

"Oh, it's quite a well-established scheme,'' Kimura said, cheered by Hara's admission of ignorance. "It was started at least seven or eight years ago when the Europeans were moaning about the adverse trade balance and our restrictive import practices. Somebody in our Ministry

24

of International Trade and Industry pointed out that it might have something to do with the fact that there are many thousands of Japanese business people living and working and exploring the markets in Europe but no more than a few hundred Europeans bothering to do the same here. There followed the usual stuff about the cultural and language barriers, and to cut a long story short, I suppose MITI and our Foreign Ministry had enough of a guilty conscience to put up some money. Anyway, they sat down with the European Community diplomats in Tokyo and worked out an arrangement whereby every year a few dozen selected young business people from the various member countries come here from Europe for several months of intensive Japanese language instruction. Then they have an equal period of familiarisation attachments to commercial or industrial enterprises here. The idea being that they then go home again and tell their parent companies where they've been going wrong in trying to sell to Japan.''

''And Marianna van Wijk was one of these,'' Hara said, nodding solemnly. ''I agree, it really is most odd, Inspector. I can hardly believe that MITI and the Foreign Ministry would have directed her to the kind of enterprise housed in the Hinomaru Building, much less on a Sunday.''

Kimura glanced suspiciously at Hara, but detected no trace of sarcasm in his manner. ''A fair surmise,'' he agreed after a brief hesitation. ''Though if I know him the Chief might well argue that it would be typical of some of our bureaucrats. As a matter of fact I think the attachments are arranged by the Federation of Economic Organisations in Tokyo. I shall have a copy of her complete programme in Japan when the papers arrive tomorrow. Meantime all we have to go on so far as she's concerned is what little we've been told over the phone, and the passport photo in her Alien Registration Card. The people living around are all being interviewed but needless to say nobody so far admits to having set eyes on her. Indeed I gather it's quite a job to get them to admit to any knowledge of the very existence of the Hinomaru Building.''

Hara nodded judiciously. "Inspector Noguchi predicted that this would be the case."

"Ninja's talking to the *yakuza* mob, is he?"

"In a sense, yes. That is to say, he is basing himself temporarily at East Central divisional headquarters, but concentrating on low-level contacts. Superintendent Otani has decided to see the Hinomaru boss personally, and to talk to the insurance company when their technical investigators have drawn up their report and discussed it with the fire brigade."

"He told you that himself, did he?" It was late on Monday afternoon, but Kimura had not himself seen Otani since the previous week, and there was resentment in his voice. "I'm surprised he's set all this up without some sort of conference. He's forever lecturing us about proper co-ordination of effort, but nobody seems to be keeping me in the picture."

"It *is* confusing," Hara agreed sympathetically, hard put to it to keep a straight face. Noguchi had not only predicted accurately the reluctance of people living in the neighbourhood of the Hinomaru Building to cooperate with the police in their enquiries following the fire, but had also treated Hara that morning to a surprisingly lifelike impersonation of Kimura complaining about the decisions Otani had made without involving him in preliminary consultations. "But I understand that the Superintendent wants to wait until the facts of the case are clearer before speculating about the Dutch woman's presence in the building."

Hara was himself more than a little perturbed by Otani's insistence that for the present the discovery of the photograph in the dead woman's bag should go unreported and that even Kimura should not be told about it. Such blatant disregard of the rules about potential evidence was most irregular, and after Otani had finally left for home the previous day even Noguchi had persuaded Hara only with great difficulty to agree to keep quiet about the picture for the time being.

"Ha! That'll be the day! I've known the Chief a great deal longer than you have, Hara. I'd be willing to bet my summer bonus against yours that he's already worked out at least three theories, all of them hopelessly wide of the mark. He reads too many detective novels, you know . . .''

The Case Of The Silenced Witness might make a good title, Otani was thinking, or perhaps *Murder By Accident*, and then gave his head an irritated little shake, angry with himself for indulging in such whimsicalities, even though they did give him a few moments' respite from his nagging anxiety over the mystery of the photograph. When Noguchi had first handed it to him his reaction had been one of simple amazement. Later something very like a superstitious dread had seized his consciousness, killing his appetite for the evening meal Hanae had prepared and making him terse and contrary with her when she tried to make conversation. Why on earth would a foreign woman want to take a picture of a perfectly ordinary Japanese family enjoying a day out at the funfair? They obviously represented three generations but there was nothing very special about that.

As Tomita edged the car through the heavy Monday traffic on the way back to headquarters Otani tried to see the situation through the eyes of his cosmopolitan friend Ambassador Atsugi of the Osaka Liaison Office of the Ministry of Foreign Affairs. It was something he did from time to time when he suspected that he might be reacting too stodgily to situations involving foreigners.

"Nothing perplexing about it, my dear Otani-san," he could imagine Atsugi saying. "Foreign visitors always like to take pictures of the natives to show people at home. She probably saw you as typical inscrutable orientals, stuffed to the eyebrows with raw fish and seaweed." Otani manfully contemplated the idea, but it wouldn't do. If she really had wanted a photo of that kind—perhaps of the happy little boy for whose pleasure the outing had been undertaken—why not ask them to pose properly as a Japanese photography buff would certainly have done? Why snap them furtively, and from an unsuitable angle? "They call them candid camera shots," the voice in his mind suggested helpfully. "Perhaps she was putting together a magazine article about the leisure boom in Japan?" No,

27

that wouldn't do either. It was a Polaroid instant print, quite unsuitable for reproduction.

"Beg pardon, sir?"

"What is it, Tomita?"

"Oh. My mistake. I thought you said something to me, sir."

Otani cleared his throat noisily and sat a little more upright. If he had got to the stage of talking to himself something must be done about it, and he forced himself to review in his mind the salient points of the thoroughly unsatisfactory conversation he had just had with Ikuo Motoyama, boss of the Hinomaru faction of one of the larger gangs which made up the mighty Yamamoto-gumi, which for all the schisms eroding its structure since the death of its last undisputed supreme head was still the dominant organised crime network in western Japan. He had never come across Motoyama before, and even though the East Central divisional inspector who set up the meeting and accompanied him had provided a lively description over the telephone in advance Otani had still been startled at first sight of the man.

Like all other very large, institutionalised organisations, the Yamamoto-gumi had a certain amount of dead wood at various managerial levels, but over the years Otani had on the whole been impressed by the quality of those of the men at or near the top whom he had met or had other opportunities to assess. His considered opinion was that the late patriarch had been mad, but nevertheless the old man had unquestionably had style. Otani would never forget the austerely but exquisitely appointed Japanese-style room in which years earlier he had once been received, or the young maidservant dressed and made up in the style of a Court lady of another age. Then again, the members of what they themselves referred to as the "presidium" who had contended for the succession after the dignified passing through natural causes of the supreme boss had all been able and resourceful, even though the two strongest among them were still several years later at loggerheads. Ikuo Motoyama was admittedly a notch or two down the hierarchy, and after a disagreeable twenty-five minutes with him at one of the larger and more expensive of Kobe's many Chinese restaurants Otani had serious doubts about his promotion prospects even in the currently still fluid situation.

In appearance Motoyama was as vulgarly ostentatious as the decor and furnishings of the private room in which he had been waiting for Otani and his companion. He was probably about fifty, Otani thought, and twenty years earlier very likely weighed twenty kilos less. Then his squat build had probably given him an air of toughness and menace; now he was physically simply repulsive. There was a sheen of sweat on his face, and his effusive but uneasy smile of welcome revealed an evil collection of brown stumps and gold teeth. Even though Otani had kept his distance and done no more than incline his head a fraction of an inch in response to Motoyama's strenuous but unsuccessful attempts to bow low, the foulness of the gangster's breath alone would have disposed Otani to cut the discussion short, however revealing it might have been.

There was of course never any question of his accepting the man's repeated offers to call for the rarest and most expensive gourmet treats the establishment could provide and sitting down with him and his two glowering minders, neither of whom uttered a word from beginning to end of the meeting. This was as unproductive as DI Urabe had predicted it would be when Otani telephoned him from home the previous evening and instructed him over his careful but sustained advice to the contrary to organise it.

Why, Motoyama greasily begged to be informed, would a law-abiding, hard-working businessman like himself even contemplate such a heinous crime as arson? No, he had not the remotest idea how the fire might have started. An electrical fault, perhaps? Yes, of course the Hinomaru Building was insured against fire; but no financial compensation could possibly meet the appalling cost to the Hinomaru group of companies of the chaos and loss of business attendant upon the disaster. Yes, of course the premises were customarily deserted on a Sunday, like the vast majority of other office

29

buildings in Kobe, the staff no doubt enjoying the innocent pleasures of family life as salarymen and office ladies are accustomed to do at weekends. Washing the car, shopping in the big department stores, or perhaps picnicking in some conveniently accessible beauty spot.

In the face of the mounting anger Otani made no attempt to conceal Motoyama conceded that he himself had the previous day visited the Kashiwara Shrine in Nara Prefecture with other members of the Hyogo branch of the All-Nippon Patriotic Anti-Communist League, and that by an odd coincidence most of his companions were in fact members of his staff. The outing had amounted to the best part of a full day trip, and no doubt the Kashiwara Shrine office staff would be pleased to endorse his statement, since they would recall that he had paid for the services of priests and attendant shrine virgins to offer ritual prayers for the well-being of the Imperial Family and for the peace and security of the nation.

"The Kashiwara priests are used to right-wing loonies, of course," Divisional Inspector Urabe had commented before seeing Otani into his car outside the restaurant, "and they'll no doubt confirm his personal alibi. With due respect, I was a bit surprised you didn't raise the matter of the foreign woman, sir. I'm afraid I did when I eventually got through on the phone to Motoyama last night. All sorts of people saw the stretcher loaded into that ambulance, after all. Obviously Motoyama denied all knowledge of her existence . . . I'd have rather liked to ask him again this morning and watch his face when he answered." Urabe shrugged. "Ah well, it can wait. I can quite see you've got more urgent things on your mind. The media, for one. They'll need careful handling."

Inspector Urabe was a seasoned, middle-aged officer whose opinions Otani knew to be worth taking seriously, and he pondered his parting words as Tomita stopped the car outside the shabby old headquarters building and scuttled out to open the door for him. The DI was quite right: the media would obviously have to be told something, but Otani wasn't at all sure what. The one thing that must certainly be

30

kept from them if at all possible at this stage was the conclusion of the pathologist who carried out the post-mortem that Marianna van Wijk had been pregnant at the time of her death.

Chapter 4

"**W**ELL, WE OBVIOUSLY HAD TO PUT OUT SOME SORT of statement," Otani said to Hanae late that evening as he stood bare-footed in his yukata at the open window of the upstairs room in which they slept and which doubled as a formal reception room on the rare occasions they received guests who had to be treated with ceremony. The rainy season was officially over but it had become increasingly muggy during the course of the day, and Hanae thought she saw a flicker of lightning in the leaden sky over in the direction of Awaji Island in the Inland Sea.

"Kimura and Hara worked it out with the Foreign Ministry liaison staff in Osaka. Just to the effect that an office building was destroyed by fire yesterday, but since it was a Sunday there were fortunately very few people about. One casualty, a foreign national who will not be named until next of kin have been informed. Rather specious, but not altogether unreasonable in the circumstances, and everybody's hoping that the papers will lose interest in a few days. It seems that neither the Dutch Embassy nor some sort of diplomatic office the European Community has in Tokyo want any speculation about what this young woman was doing in a *yakuza* headquarters building in the first place. Though that, of course, is precisely what we're most anxious to find out." He sighed and pulled the front of his yukata open a little more, fanning himself with a flat paper fan which, with a hand-towel, had been presented as a midsummer gift by the proprietor of their local sake shop. It bore an advertisement for the locally produced Hakutsuru brand sake, which the Otanis seldom chose.

"It's an awful thing to say, but I suppose that if that other dreadful fire had to happen at all, it was just as well from your point of view that it coincided. The one at the hotel in the hot-spring resort, I mean." In spite of the sticky closeness of the atmosphere Hanae shivered a little at her own cynicism before moving over to put a fresh chemically-treated pad in the anti-mosquito gadget on the tatami matting and plug it in.

Otani nodded. "Yes, that's certainly grabbed all the headlines today. Our local mystery can hardly compete with over thirty dead and almost as many in hospital. We shall have a bit more background information tomorrow. Some papers are being sent down from Tokyo. Though I can't for the life of me imagine how we're going to set about the problem if that Motoyama creature was telling the truth when he told Inspector Urabe he'd never heard of the woman and hadn't the remotest idea how she came to be in the building. I wish I'd asked him myself now."

Otani felt tetchy and out of sorts at the end of a thoroughly unsatisfactory evening which he realised was probably due to his own reticence. Forthcoming with Hanae about every other aspect of the case, he had still said nothing to her about the photograph which, against all the rules, he had kept in his possession. He was sure she had guessed he was keeping something from her, because Hanae could always tell when he had something personal on his mind. Usually he saw her working hard to pretend otherwise. It was harder when she reacted politely but coolly, distancing herself emotionally until such time as he saw fit to readmit her into his confidence. Her present attitude was even more difficult for him to cope with in that she seemed neither tactfully sympathetic

33

nor hurt but merely distracted, as though she had more important things to think about.

"I'm sure you'll think of something," Hanae said unhelpfully as she opened the big cupboard briskly and took out the two heavy futons which constituted the basis of their bedding. Laying them side by side directly on the tatami she shook out the bottom sheet and Otani absent-mindedly helped her to spread it smoothly over the futon and tuck it under the edges. The two hard little pillows followed next, and finally the lightweight double duvet they used in summer, already in its own fitted, washable cover.

"Thank you for the compliment," Otani said tartly, still offended by Hanae's matter-of-fact attitude, and went back to the window for his habitual last look over the built-up area to the lights of the ships far away in the great bay while his wife inserted herself neatly under the covers. She remained silent, and after a few moments he stripped off his yukata and rolled into bed beside her with a little cough as the fumes from the mosquito repellent caught at his throat. The smell was both sickly sweet and vaguely antiseptic; not as pleasant as the aroma from the old-fashioned smouldering coils which could still be bought at hardware shops but were, he supposed, rather messy and less efficient.

Otani thought his prospects of getting to sleep seemed very remote, and his spirits sagged at the thought that Hanae was probably just as wide awake, lying there a few inches away with nothing to say for herself, the pair of them staring up at the old wooden ceiling like a couple of ill-tempered children mulishly not speaking to each other.

"What I should really like to do," he said experimentally after taking a deep breath, "is make love, but I suppose . . ." No response. "No, well, I thought probably not."

Nothing. He could hardly even hear her breathing as he tried again, his mood of self-pity deepening by the second. "Look, I'm sorry I snapped at you like that; but I've got rather a lot on my mind."

"You're not the only one, you know." Hanae's muttered response was in any case subdued, and since as she spoke she was flouncing over on to her side to face away from him Otani wasn't at all sure that he had heard aright.

"What's the matter, Ha-chan?" he demanded in sudden alarm, raising himself up on one elbow. Hanae's shoulder and the back of her head were dimly visible against the pale sheet and pillow-case. "Are you all right? I mean, you're not ill, are you?"

At this Hanae rolled back over again, and Otani was relieved to see a rueful little smile flicker briefly over her face. "No, no. I'm not ill," she said with a hint of warmth returning to her voice.

"But you've got something on your mind," he insisted. "You just said so. Tell me about it. Perhaps I can help."

Hanae sighed. "I did tell you about it. Before the weekend. I don't suppose you even remember."

Otani gazed down at her, trying hard to think back, and after a few seconds dredged up a recollection of something Hanae had rather gone on about over supper several evenings previously. "You're not still bothered about this idea of Akira's to grow cucumbers, are you?"

"Tomatoes. I said you hadn't remembered."

"Tomatoes then, same thing. Oh, really, Ha-chan! Don't take it so seriously. It's just some wild notion that's seized his fancy for a while. Probably a bit unsettled after the move back from London, but he's much too sensible to do anything silly. I expect he's thought better of it already, and even if he hasn't he soon will once he starts doing a few calculations, quite apart from anything Akiko has to say on the subject. It isn't like you to get into a state over something like that."

"I'm sorry. Perhaps I am being silly, but . . . things aren't right between them. I'm sure of it."

Hanae lay still, a little comforted by her husband's reassurances even as the vivid recollection of the embrace she had observed near Osaka Station a few days earlier came back into her mind. In a way she wished she had told him about it at once, yet paradoxically was glad she hadn't. Prurient gossip was not in her line, and she even tended to change the subject quite soon when Otani came home with some scandalous titbit about bachelor Inspector Kimura's exotic love life. That kiss *could* after all have signified little. Hanae had not been much in the company of foreigners, but during her one and only overseas trip she had been startled by the uninhibited behaviour even of the English who were reputed to be so reserved and dignified, and had noticed how much more extroverted both Akiko and her husband had become during their years in London.

In any case, even her beloved Tetsuo would very possibly laugh it off as being of no account if she did tell him. Japanese of their generation had been brought up to regard casual male infidelity as being of small, if any, consequence. Over the years Hanae had occasionally considered the possibility that her husband might himself have sampled the attractions of other women, only to put the idea firmly out of her mind. It was more than enough that she was sure that he had never had a serious love affair, that even at their age he still enjoyed their lovemaking, and that she could count on his protective warmth and affectionate friendship. All in all, she had no desire to hear his views on the subject of extra-marital flings.

"Well," she admitted at last, "it's not my business, I know. If they are going through a difficult patch they must sort things out in their own way." She reached out for Otani's hand and squeezed it. "I'm sorry too. I didn't really listen properly to everything you were telling me, but I can see how frustrating this case must be for you. But you did say there are a good many other young foreigners in Japan under the same scholarship scheme as this poor lady. They'd all know each other, surely? Perhaps Mr Kimura could get in touch with some of her friends and pick up a few ideas like that?"

"Yes. Yes, he could, couldn't he? That's a very good idea, Ha-chan. I'll talk to Kimura first thing in the morning."

They both retreated again into their private preoccupations, but this time the silence was companionable rather than strained, and in spite of the oppressive heat and the distant rumbling of thunder Otani drifted off to sleep rather sooner than he expected.

* * *

Some ten miles or so away in the Shimizus' bright, modern little house in Senri New Town, Akiko looked in again on her sleeping son, picked up his grubby Snoopy from the floor and replaced it beside his pillow. Then she went into the bathroom, studied her drawn face, sighed and put on some lipstick before going back downstairs to the living room where she made another attempt to interest herself in the television, but without success. The fact was that she was lonely, desolately unhappy and very worried.

Even before they went to live in London Akiko had been conscious of her good fortune in having a husband with views as advanced as Akira's had remained after his reconciliation to the capitalist system and recruitment to the junior executive staff of the company in which he was now a senior manager. Indifferent to the jibes of colleagues who teased him about belonging to the *mai-hoomu-zoku* or My Home Tribe, Akira Shimizu had from the outset steadfastly ignored the salaryman convention of spending the greater part of every evening drinking in the company of the people he worked alongside with, and instead headed for home at the end of the working day.

Before Kazuo was born the Shimizus had enjoyed plenty of evenings out together: at concerts, rehearsals of the choral society they both belonged to, the theatre and the cinema. The new baby had confined them to their flat, but even then Akira had almost always arrived home in time to lend a hand with the rituals of bathtime and bedtime, to share the evening meal with his wife and to talk afterwards rather than turning up night after night at ten or eleven half drunk to pick at some warmed-over food and then fall straight into bed. Akiko knew that her married women acquaintances of those days weren't exaggerating when they complained that they only really spoke to their husbands at weekends.

At the time Akiko thought she knew when she was well off; but then came the transfer to Europe, sudden affluence as expatriates, a luxury flat in St John's Wood and above all the liberating phenomenon of baby-sitters. It had been like a preview of the Western Paradise of the Pure Land she had heard about during the adolescent flirtation with Buddhism which preceded her conversion to Maoism. Admittedly there was in London an endless succession of visiting executives from headquarters for Akira to coddle and entertain after office hours, but they had also had all the chances anybody could want to abandon themselves to an orgy of culture and entertainment in a city which Akira said he honestly thought had almost as much to offer in that line as Tokyo itself, and cheaper.

Akiko eyed the modest collection of bottles on top of the record cabinet and yielded to the temptation to get herself another gin and tonic. It wasn't that since their return to Japan and acquisition of a new house her husband had taken to arriving home drunk. In fact he was inclined to look down his nose at her whenever—as Akiko supposed in all honesty *was* increasingly often—he let himself in and found her with a drink somewhere handy.

In other respects she hardly recognised him as the lover and friend he had been in London. For one thing, since soon after his return to work at headquarters on promotion he had evidently resigned from the My Home Tribe. He rarely put in an appearance much before nine in the evening on working days and on two or three occasions during the past month had arrived home at nearly midnight. Before the new pattern became established Akiko had now and then cheerfully asked what he had been up to, quite ready to sympathise if he had been unable to escape from boring business acquaintances, but after a few evenings of being shut out of his confidence and in effect told to mind her own business she had taken refuge in a sullen silence of her own, punctuated only by the ill-tempered banging of pots and pans in the kitchen.

She finished her drink and replenished the glass, hardly noticing that she did so. She knew she had become short-tempered with her husband, but then he for his part had been displaying some of the worst characteristics of what she thought of as a typical Japanese husband. The Akira who had always had plenty to say for himself and delighted in a lively discussion on almost any subject under the sun had been replaced by a taciturn, unhelpful stranger, grumbling if he couldn't at once put a hand on a freshly ironed shirt, and seemingly so wrapped up in his own affairs that he was quite willing to leave Kazuo's upbringing and education entirely in her hands.

That was why, extraordinary and impracticable as the whole notion sounded to Akiko, she had listened with a sense of burgeoning relief to his enthusiastic description of the fabulous tomato plant he had seen at the Science Expo and his vision of a new way of life for them through "hyponica culture". She thought it most unlikely to happen, but for a week or two Akira did seem to have been jolted out of his trough of uncommunicativeness, and Akiko for her part had no intention of acting as a wet blanket.

Then came the weekend. Akira was very late home on Friday and went out without a word on Saturday morning, leaving her to try after a couple of hours to explain to a crushed, disbelieving Kazuo that his *Oto-chan* was very busy and wasn't after all able to take him to the Children's Science Centre as he had promised. Angry, fearful and bewildered, Akiko took the little boy herself. The outing was not a success, and when they arrived home again Akiko found a note from her husband on the kitchen table. It was terse and to the point: an important business contact had arrived in Tokyo and he had to go and see him there. He doubted if he would have a chance to ring her, but would in any case be back on Monday evening.

The headache which had been nagging at Akiko all day was much worse, and she put her glass down carefully and closed her eyes for a moment. When she opened them again she felt disoriented, her mouth sour and dry, and she gaped for a moment uncomprehendingly at the hissing snowstorm of the blank television screen before turning to look at the clock. It was a quarter to three in the morning, and Akira had not come home.

Chapter 5

"**G**OOD-LOOKING WOMAN," KIMURA SAID APPRECIA-tively, studying the cutting again. It was from an *Asahi Journal* dated a few weeks earlier: a half-page black and white photograph accompanying an article about the European Business Study Fellowship Scheme, showing some of the current batch of Fellows being greeted by the aged President of the Federation of Economic Organisations at its plush Tokyo headquarters building. The caption gave the names, nationalities and ages of the visitors and explained that the rising young European managers had completed their intensive Japanese language course and were about to set off to various cities in Japan to observe Japanese industrial and commercial practice at first hand. "Taller than any of the others, men and women alike. And the President barely comes up to her bosom."

"She's dead, Inspector." Hara's voice was quiet and un-inflected as he took the proffered cutting, but it cut its way into Kimura's consciousness and he had the grace to look embarrassed. "Yes. Yes, indeed she is. I hadn't forgotten. Not that there was ever much doubt about the identification, but the photocopy of the dentist's notes on her clinches it, according to the path lab. Just as well she asked the consular people at the Netherlands Embassy to recommend one when her filling came loose.''

''And very efficient on their part to remember. This magazine cutting came from the EC Delegation office, though, I believe?''

''Yes. With copies of her original fellowship application and her professional programme in Japan. They liaise with the Japanese side over the administrative details. Have you ever heard of Dejima Pharmaceuticals, Hara? It sounds as if it might have something to do with Nagasaki. Isn't there a Dejima district there?''

''Quite right. Of great historical importance.'' Hara sounded surprised that Kimura had heard of it. ''I don't recall having heard of a pharmaceutical company of that name while I was there, though.''

Kimura rubbed his nose and pushed the open manila folder in Hara's direction. ''The study tour programme's on top. Marianna van Wijk ended a six-week attachment to Dejima Pharmaceuticals in Osaka last week. Their head office, presumably. That's the nearest her itinerary brought her to here. Otherwise apart from Tokyo she was supposed to go to Kawasaki and Fukuoka. Fukuoka this week, actually. Needless to say the people there have been told the attachment's off.''

''But not why, I presume.''

''Right. Anyway, Kawasaki and Fukuoka are both a long way outside the Hinomaru gang's sphere of activity, according to Ninja. Though they have their links with other outfits up and down the country, of course.'' Kimura placed both hands flat on the surface of his tidy little desk and levered himself to his feet. ''Well, got to start somewhere. I think I'll give these Dejima people a ring and find out what they thought about Miss van Wijk. Or slip over to Osaka and have a word with their personnel manager.''

Hara blinked several times, took off his glasses and polished them with unnecessary vigour. ''You'll inform the Osaka prefectural force first, I presume?''

Kimura gazed at him with tolerant amusement. ''Er, no. I don't believe I'll bother them, Hara. I'm not proposing to arrest the man. The case against him is far from complete.''

Feeling rather pleased with a shaft of wit he thought worthy of Otani himself, Kimura winked at his colleague and went to the door. "Take your time over those papers. Let Migishima have the folder next door when you've finished, will you? He'll copy anything you'd like to keep by you." Then he breezed away, and after shaking his head slowly more in sorrow than in disapproval Hara gave his full attention to the folder of papers assembled by the Tokyo police with the co-operation of the staff of the Netherlands Embassy and the European Community Delegation there.

Apart from the *Asahi Journal* cutting everything was in English, which Hara could read with comparative ease even though he would never have ventured to speak it in Kimura's presence. Marianna van Wijk seemed to have been an impressively qualified person. Born in Utrecht, she had studied Far Eastern history and languages at Leiden University before being snapped up as a management trainee in the marketing division of a leading manufacturer of electrical goods. Three years later her employers had been enlightened enough to send her to the London Business School where she had won a place on the MBA course: Hara sighed as he reminded himself that all educated people in the Netherlands have the ability to handle English effortlessly without regarding it as much of an accomplishment. By the time Marianna applied for her Japan Business Study Fellowship she was an assistant marketing director of her company, controlling a considerable chunk of a multi-million-dollar advertising budget. Small wonder she hadn't married, Hara reflected as he looked again at the tall woman in the magazine picture.

There were eight Europeans in their late twenties or early thirties in the picture, three of them women who each in their different ways looked impressive; more so than the men, Hara thought, but that could have been simply because they *were* women. *Tonderu onna* or female flyers were becoming enough of a phenomenon in Japanese business and professional circles for the phrase to have entered everyday speech, but judging from the politely appalled expression the photographer had captured on the face of the *Keidanren* president they were uncommon visitors to his luxurious sanctum.

The tall blonde for her part looked thoroughly at ease and even slightly amused, and reminded Hara very slightly of a younger version of the British Princess Alexandra by whom he had been much smitten as a boy when she visited Japan and appeared frequently in the television news bulletins. He shook his head and closed the folder sadly. It was hard to credit that Marianna van Wijk had any reason to be inside the Hinomaru Building at any time, much less alone when it was otherwise deserted and about to be set on fire either by its owners or by their enemies.

That it had been a case of arson was now established beyond question. A certain amount of ingenuity had been involved in rigging the main time-switch so that a pre-arranged electrical fault would trigger off a fire in the central air-conditioning system; but not enough to fool the insurance company's investigators or the fire brigade's own specialists. The question was whether the local boss Motoyama had himself arranged for it to be done in order to realise a great deal of cash or—and this was a subtler hypothesis suggested by Noguchi—whether it had been arranged by a rival group learning of Motoyama's proposed pilgrimage with his henchmen to the right-wingers'' favourite Shinto shrine in the region and the resulting vulnerability of his headquarters. Noguchi theorised that at one stroke Motoyama's enemies could destroy his physical base of operations and, by leaving just enough indications of arson, deprive him of the insurance money while facing criminal charges into the bargain.

Hara knew that Noguchi was currently busy tapping into his vast and delicately balanced network of informers in the quest for pointers, and that he would be unlikely to be seeing much of him for a day or two, unless the old bruiser were to drop in unexpectedly at the Hara home. He had developed the habit of doing so now and then soon after Hara had been transferred from Nagasaki and been taken under his wing to the bemusement of both Otani and Kimura. Nothing would ever induce Hara to reveal to a soul that Noguchi liked to read his little daughter bedtime stories or that she adored him and called him Fat Grandad.

The overt police operation mounted by his department in

collaboration with East Central division's own small criminal investigation section and the uniformed men attached to the *koban* or neighbourhood police box with oversight of the Hinomaru Building was still being frustrated by what amounted to a wall of silence. Not one of the local residents so far approached admitted to having seen anybody enter or leave the building on the day of the fire, or to knowing anything about its owners or occupants. Hara had not given up hope of finding some gossipy old lady in the neighbourhood with nothing much to do all day except keep an eye on comings and goings, but visits had been made to virtually every household within a radius of three blocks and there weren't a great many left to be covered.

It was beyond doubt that the people living in closest proximity to the gangster headquarters must know what sort of people frequented the place, and equally clear that they either preferred not to think about them or had reason to believe that it was in their interests to keep quiet. None of them had quite managed to deny that a fire had taken place at all, but a high proportion had claimed that while it was going on they had been shopping or visiting friends in quite another part of the city. Hara knew other ways of persuading reluctant witnesses to come forward and realised that it would certainly be necessary to interview some of the local residents for a second time, but both temperamentally and intellectually he favoured the gentle approach and still hoped that subtlety in dealing with people who were probably wholly innocent and at worst guilty of nothing more than excessive prudence would yield results.

Hara closed the folder, unwound his ungainly body and went into the adjoining room to hand the papers back to Kimura's personal assistant, Migishima.

Between perms Hanae took care of her own hair. She listened with politely suppressed amazement when friends and acquaintances she met at the western-style cookery classes held at the Kobe YWCA spoke of going to the beauty shop once a week to have theirs done. The Otanis were comfortably enough off these days, but their pleasures were simple and

44

they were largely immune to the general Japanese mania for conspicuous consumption. In this they were most unlike their nearest neighbours the Kobayashis. Mr and Mrs Kobayashi were not all that much younger than Hanae and her husband. Yet they lived in a frenzy of acquisitiveness, giving perfectly serviceable equipment to the "special garbage" collector month after month to make way for the newest models in the way of television sets, video recorders, microwave ovens, washing machines and air-conditioners. Although to the best of Hanae's knowledge totally unmusical, they had recently had a huge piano delivered . . . at suppertime of course so that everybody in the street would know.

So Hanae could easily have afforded a fortnightly or even weekly trip to the *Montmartre* salon in the huge underground Sanchika Town shopping centre in Kobe, but the frugal habits of a lifetime were not easily overridden, and in any case she told herself that she enjoyed it all the more when she did go every three or four months.

It was particularly soothing that day, when she was still nervy and feeling at odds with life, worried about the Shimizus and more obscurely concerned about her husband, to lean backwards almost horizontally in the chair, close her eyes and surrender herself to the ministering hands of the deferential girl in the pink smock. She was no more than a slip of a thing, but her fingers were strong and confident as they massaged Hanae's scalp through the slick foam of the shampoo and then, later, worked at the tense muscles of her neck and shoulders. Even the warm cocktail of perfumes which saturated the atmosphere and normally left Hanae feeling slightly queasy seemed comfortingly, securely feminine that day, and by the time the bright plastic rollers were in place and she was safely installed under the dryer she felt more relaxed and cheerful than she had for a long time.

There was enough reading matter at her side for a world cruise, and Hanae glanced first through the current issue of *Family Graphic*. It was her favourite glossy monthly, and its mouth-watering recipe pages and impeccably photographed interiors and fashions beguiled her as usual. Then she tuttutted briefly over the cheap mass-market *Weekly Post*, a sensational fudge of gossip about political and television personalities and articles about sumo wrestling, astrology, new cosmetics and other popular preoccupations such as the bust measurements of the hostesses to be found in a selection of bars in Tokyo's Roppongi district. Liberally illustrated with nudes, cartoons and advertisements for everything from cameras and home computers to cures for baldness and impotence, the *Weekly Post* and its more or less interchangeable competitors offered a kaleidoscopic view of a world of which Hanae knew little and about which she cared not at all, yet one which differed only in superficial inessentials from that of the better-off townspeople of Osaka or Edo two or three hundred years earlier.

There was an *Asahi Journal* further down the pile and Hanae riffled through its much more sober pages, settling down with a sense of something like relief as the girl deftly removed her rollers to a thoughtful interview with a woman member of the National Diet about the problems facing the Japanese educational system. Unfortunately though this soon made her start worrying about little Kazuo all over again, and when she turned the page and saw a photograph of the foreign woman she had seen kissing her son-in-law Hanae she became very pale and her hands shook a little.

The beautician noticed and asked solicitously if Hanae felt all right. Hanae recovered enough composure to smile at her wanly and nod, before concentrating during the finishing touches of a hairdo to which she had become completely oblivious on the article which accompanied the photograph.

Hanae arrived home eventually with very little recollection of having made her way to the Hankyu Line station, bought a ticket, taken a stopping train to Rokko and walked up the hill with some Chinese cabbage and three hundred grams of chicken breast she seemed to have acquired on the way. Still functioning almost automatically she made herself some green tea and drank a cup, accompanied by two rice crackers. Then she stared at the telephone for some time, wondering whether she should ring her husband at his office. Over the years Hanae had so rarely felt justified in doing such a thing that she had never memorised the numbers either of the headquarters switchboard or of his private line, perhaps because Otani made her keep a note of them in her purse.

After much deliberation and several changes of mind she finally decided to wait until he came home to confirm that the name printed in phonetic *katakana* characters in the caption under the photograph of the tall woman and her European colleagues really was the same as the one her Tetsuo had mentioned when telling her about the identification of the body found in the burnt-out Hinomaru Building. There was a hit-or-miss quality about the rendering of many names in the characters reserved for foreign words. There was no difficulty about "Marianna" which went perfectly into Japanese sounds, but her husband had after all only tried to get his tongue round what he pronounced as "Ban Waiku or something" once.

Hanae nearly jumped out of her skin when the phone rang.

Chapter 6

"SHE SOUNDED REASONABLY CALM," HANAE SAID THE moment Otani arrived home. He forced a smile.

"So do you," he said as he slipped his shoes off and stepped up from the stone floor of the little entrance hall to the polished wood and tatami matting beyond. "Reasonably." Then he bent and raised her to her feet, since as always Hanae had without conscious thought sunk to her knees to greet him.

When he put his arms round her Hanae wanted to weep. This was something she had very rarely allowed herself to do even in private since the childhood during which she had as a respectable middle-class girl been schooled to suppress signs of emotion, even of the joyful variety—though patriotic fervour had of course been quite in order in the wartime years of her puberty. She therefore did no more than rest her head for a moment on her husband's shoulder before taking a deep breath and releasing herself from his gentle embrace.

"Husbands have been known to stay out all night before now," Otani said as he followed Hanae into the all-purpose ground-floor room and flopped down on to the nearest *zabuton* cushion. It was a limp remark and he knew it deserved no better a response than the brief glance of irritation she

48

flashed in his direction. "I came as soon as I could get away," he added. "Would you like me to go over there with you?"

Hanae shook her head. "No. I'll go on my own. I can take care of Kazuo-chan and let her get some rest. That will probably do her more good than anything until she gets word of some kind from Akira. But I must talk to you properly first. Your supper's almost ready . . . I shall have something with Akiko later. Come into the kitchen, will you?"

A creature of habit, Otani liked to take his bath immediately after arriving home in the evening, put on a yukata and watch one of the network news programmes on television before enjoying his meal at leisure and in Hanae's company in the living room. The prospect of having it right away at the kitchen table while Hanae bustled about at the cooker and sink before going over to the Shimizu house and leaving him to his own devices did nothing to cheer him, but he got up again obediently and trailed after her.

"You say she's been in touch with his office?"

"Yes. Well, unofficially, of course. She rang one of his assistants there. A Mr Taniguchi. She didn't want to talk to Akira's secretary, another woman would have noticed at once how worried she was, but this Mr Taniguchi thinks of nothing but baseball."

"And?" Otani cut in before Hanae could expand on the character and interests of Akira's colleague. He knew her well enough to realise that in rambling on she was putting off telling him something important and would in normal circumstances have quite enjoyed teasing it out of her, but he was in an edgy, impatient mood.

"It's only fried rice. I'm sorry," she said, putting a bowlful in front of him. In fact Hanae's fried rice was usually a creative masterpiece garnished with all manner of good things, but something she seldom prepared in summertime. On this occasion it provided further evidence that her thoughts were elsewhere.

Otani tried again. "What did this Taniguchi tell Akiko?"

"Well, she'd begun by saying that she knew Akira was on a business trip and didn't like to bother him, but that something had come up which meant she needed to get in touch with him urgently and wondered if he'd left a note of his whereabouts. Mr Taniguchi couldn't help. He said he hadn't heard about any business trip, but that he'd check with Miss Shiromoto—that's Akira's secretary. Then Miss Shiromoto came on the line herself which was the last thing Akiko wanted, and said that she'd been about to ring to ask if Akira was sick. He'd missed an important meeting, apparently. So now of course it's all over the office that his wife hasn't the slightest idea where he is.''

Otani prodded about in the bowl with his chopsticks and found a piece of chicken which he chewed thoughtfully as he looked so fixedly into Hanae's eyes that she turned away from him.

''It's worrying, of course,'' he said, noting the pink flush of her throat and cheeks. ''He might really have been taken ill, I suppose. At least I'm in a good position to have a word with people in the Osaka force and have hospitals and clinics checked. If Akiko-chan would like me to. Tokyo too, if that's where he said he was going on Saturday. There's something else on your mind, though. Isn't there, Ha-chan? Hadn't you better tell me before you go?''

It was getting on for eight by the time Otani walked slowly back up the hill after seeing Hanae to the station. He visualised her sitting in the Osaka-bound train on her way to their daughter's side, brooding over the implications of the photograph he had at last shown her. He hoped the two women would discuss the subject, however painful it might be for Akiko to accept that her husband had been at the very least on terms of affectionate friendship with the young Dutchwoman whose body had been found in the burnt-out headquarters of a *yakuza* faction in Kobe. At least with luck she could be spared the knowledge that Marianna van Wijk had been pregnant with what she would inevitably be convinced must be the child of her husband Akira.

All that the belated pooling of his and Hanae's information had produced so far was a plausible explanation of the dead woman's possession of the photograph, but Otani felt oddly relieved by it. He could hardly expect Hanae or Akiko to see it that way, but he found it quite touching to think that Marianna van Wijk had gone to the extreme of tailing them all to the funfair and furtively taking a photograph of the man she must have been in love with. Nevertheless the fact remained that his son-in-law had abruptly disappeared on Saturday, and that the woman Hanae had seen embracing him publicly in Osaka and who carried his photograph in her handbag had been found dead in inexplicable circumstances on Sunday. Otani was not altogether sorry that he would have the house to himself for the night and conceivably longer, because he had some serious thinking to do.

Not long before his mother-in-law arrived at his house and was admitted by his distraught wife Akira Shimizu clenched his fists on his thighs and glared in impotent defiance at Makoto Aoki. "A single short phone call. Or even a note by post. That's all I'm asking," he pleaded. "Can't I at least let my wife know I'm still alive? She'll be desperately worried by now." His mental agony was the only thing which in a paradoxical way seemed to dull the physical pain which racked his lower body after he had been forced to kneel immobile for over an hour on the bare wooden floor while Aoki reviled and insulted him.

"You always were a sentimental bastard, Shimizu.' Aoki's voice was harsh and his manner brutally uncompromising. "With a lot of luck she'll see you again eventually. If you both still want that when all this is over. But only if she's kept totally in the dark until then. You damn fool, we *want* her ringing round the hospitals, setting up a hue and cry after you. If there's anything in this preposterous tale of yours." He laughed. It was an ugly sound, grating and devoid of mirth or humanity. "You're a typical bourgeois husband, aren't you? Timid, cowardly, but at the mercy of your balls. Nice little arrangement, screwing around and nobody the wiser till your current bit of skirt gets murdered. For all I know you did it yourself. You say not. You say you know who did. Why should I believe you? Why should I care one way or the other? It's not that important, the girl can't be brought back to life. You're rotten with guilt anyway and with

51

good reason. So you 'evaporate', like thousands of others every year in this capitalist collectivist paradise of Japan—''

"One day I'm going to kill you, Aoki." Shimizu's voice was flat, his words given greater force by its very lack of expression, and Aoki raised an eyebrow.

"I doubt if you've got the guts. Your wife might not approve. Then again, she might, I suppose. I always thought she might be the Lady Macbeth type . . . but that's by the way. For the time being you're here. And you're going to do exactly what I tell you. Aren't you, Comrade Shimizu?''

Shimizu rocked to one side under the impact of a stinging slap on the face, and at once the pain lying in wait in his lower limbs exploded to dominate his consciousness.

"No. I'm going to kill you," he managed to whisper, and Aoki hit him again. Shimizu lost count of the number of times the question was bellowed into his face and he returned the same answer; but at last something seemed to snap in his mind and almost without realising it he bowed humbly in submission. He could do nothing about the tears which streamed down his cheeks.

Chapter 7

"**T**HEN I REALISED THAT THE LINK COULD DATE FROM my son-in-law's time in London," Otani went on. "According to the information given in her scholarship application form. I don't know if you'd agree, Kimura, but it occurs to me that while she was studying there she might already have been thinking in terms of coming to Japan and approached any Japanese businessmen who might have been handy for whatever advice they could give her."

Kimura nodded judiciously. "Entirely possible," he conceded. He was still very much on his dignity, having earlier been incredulous and outraged in equal measure when Otani summoned him to his office alone and showed him the photograph while explaining that Noguchi and Hara had known about its existence since the day of the fire. It had been a difficult few minutes, but for all his formidable personal authority Otani was usually ready enough to apologise to any of his subordinates he realised he had slighted or offended in some way, and by the time Noguchi and Hara joined them his careful explanation had gradually coaxed Kimura into a less negative frame of mind.

"Well, there's little point in our speculating about it," Otani said. "It's something to keep in mind, though. My daughter might know, in any case, but I'm not at present in a position to ask her.'' He hesitated, then got up and went over to his desk. Noguchi and Kimura exchanged a glance as Otani rummaged in one of the drawers and found a Peace brand packet with a couple of dried-up cigarettes in it, took one out and lit it before returning to his usual easy-chair and looking round at what Hanae called his inner cabinet. They were all in their shirt-sleeves, Hara having been invited to take off the jacket he had arrived in. Even so their foreheads glistened and Noguchi mopped his from time to time with a handkerchief which had seen better days a long time in the past.

''The situation as I see it, gentlemen, is that there are two quite separate strands to this affair. No, three. First, a major case of arson, fairly and squarely within our jurisdiction and something which it shouldn't be beyond our wits and resources to clear up. Second, the associated death of a foreign national. At the very least by misadventure, and possibly as a result of foul play although the medical evidence doesn't point to any immediate cause of death apart from asphyxiation. Certainly in circumstances which raise a lot of questions needing answers. Third, a missing person named Akira Shimizu, who happens to be my son-in-law but who is resident in Osaka Prefecture and would in the ordinary way of things therefore be no official business of ours unless our Osaka colleagues were to ask us to help find him. On the other hand my wife is certain that quite by chance she saw him in the company of Marianna van Wijk a few days before her death, and witnessed a public display of affection between them. She could be mistaken, but knowing her as I do I personally would have doubted it, even if the dead woman's handbag had not contained a photograph of my son-in-law and the rest of the family. You look worried, Hara. Have I left something out?''

Hara's eyelids fluttered while he was shaking his head: a reaction Otani had learned to regard with caution. ''No, sir,'' he said at last. ''You have comprehensively surveyed the situation. Mrs Otani's informal testimony is particularly valuable, of course, in accounting for the photograph.'' There was a touch of colour in his normally pallid face and he busied himself cleaning his glasses.

"But what, Hara? You obviously have some reservation or other. Get it off your chest."

Hara replaced the glasses and sighed. "With all respect, sir, I wonder if . . . that is to say—"

He was interrupted by a growling rumble from Noguchi as he hauled himself into an upright position and glared at Otani. "What he's trying to tell you is that you ought to back off. Too near home. Should have thought you'd have seen that for yourself."

Otani looked into his old friend's face and saw affection and anxiety as well as irritation there. Hara still looked embarrassed but determined, while Kimura was obviously rearranging his thoughts to align himself with the others. There had, after all, been little time for the realisation of the impropriety of Otani's continuing involvement with the case to have dawned upon him. Noguchi was junior in rank but older than his commander, and this fact combined with their long association and mutual regard licensed him to be forthright. It was a privilege he rarely exercised, though, and almost never in the presence of third parties. The blunt reprimand angered Otani, who held his tongue with great difficulty as his heart raced briefly and the adrenaline surged into his bloodstream. He soon had his breathing under control again though, the monitor in his mind forcing him to acknowledge that they could be right, however much he might hate having to come to terms with the realisation.

As the silence dragged on he smoked the remainder of the dry, tasteless cigarette while conquering the temptation to overrule his colleagues peremptorily. To proceed by consensus was the Japanese way, but it was not one which had ever much appealed to Otani in times of stress. He reflected that over the years he had permitted, indeed encouraged Kimura to play an important part in several investigations involving women with whom his philandering assistant was on terms of varying degrees of personal intimacy. He had seen nothing wrong in taking advantage of Kimura's temperamental inclination to interpret the old maxim *cherchez la femme* in the most positive and thoroughgoing sense, and by this means useful information had often enough been elicited which was hardly likely to have emerged otherwise.

Kimura was a bachelor and fancy-free, though: a close family connection was something else, especially perhaps in Japan, and Kimura would be the first to point that out if Otani were to try such a line of argument. Then again, although it was hard to imagine that there could have been anything but a tragic ending to the affair, Otani still often reproached himself for not having excluded Noguchi from the fugu poisoning case of a few years back as soon as he had suspected the truth about the identity of the North Korean agent involved.

It was an agonising dilemma. Otani respected the skills of his senior associates. Yet he had a proper pride in his own ability, and who was in a better position than he to assess the nature and implications of Akira Shimizu's role in this confused tangle of events? Even as he indulged that thought, the recollection of his own grossly impaired judgments, when in another harrowing case Hanae had been kidnapped, forced itself into his consciousness and shamed him at last into grudging submission.

"I'm sorry, gentlemen," he said after the silence had dragged itself out seemingly interminably. Then he stubbed out the cigarette with deliberation before looking directly at Hara.

"Ninja's right, of course. It shouldn't have been necessary for you to feel obliged to raise the issue, Inspector, and I offer you my apologies. I can see there's a strong argument that I should withdraw from this case, at least temporarily . . . Ninja, since all three of you must clearly be involved, you'd better assume overall responsibility. Meantime I'll consider my personal position and discuss it with my wife. I suppose one of you will be wanting to take a statement from her." He looked at his watch. "Do continue the discussion here as long as necessary. I . . . it's my Rotary Club meeting today anyway. It'll make a change for me to arrive early."

The other three men all stood as he rose to his feet and went over to take the jacket of his dark grey suit off the bent wire hanger suspended from one of the ornate curlicues of the old-fashioned wooden coat and umbrella stand near the door and slip it on. Then he fumbled in one of its pockets and produced a little metal object, unscrewed its back and inserted it in his buttonhole.

"I don't bother with this as a rule," he muttered defensively. "But you have to pay a fine if you don't wear your Rotary badge at meetings. Well, I'll be getting along." He paused with his hand on the door-knob and nodded at his colleagues with an awkward little smile. "Nuisance to have to wear a suit even at this time of the year, but it'll be air-conditioned, of course. Yes. Well, we must all hope my son-in-law will show up very soon, mustn't we?" Then he was gone.

"He's upset. Whatever the rights and wrongs of it, you were a bit hard on him, Ninja," Kimura said as he flopped back into his chair. Noguchi merely grunted as he lowered his own much more considerable bulk, while Hara walked over to the window and looked out over the functional modern facilities of the container terminal dominating the harbour.

"The skyline must have been much more interesting in the old days," he said reflectively. "Cranes and derricks everywhere; much more bustle."

Kimura was affronted. "I'm glad you're enjoying the view," he said stiffly. "I should have thought it would be more productive to think about what we can do to help the Chief out. What's the matter with you two, anyway? I'm the one with a right to be annoyed, not you. You've been sitting on the information about that photo for days: I get told about it this morning. All the same I can see the old man's point of view a lot better than you, apparently. He must be worried to death."

"Simmer down, Kimura." Unusually for him when ensconced in his usual chair, Noguchi had both eyes open. "And you, Hara. Come over here and stop dithering. That's better. Got to get a few things straight. Right. We all know the commander will no more be able to keep out of this altogether than fly in the air, whatever he says. Got a perfect

57

right to help his daughter try and locate her husband anyway. Shimizu's own parents are dead.''

Hara was nodding in enthusiastic agreement. "Exactly," he put in when Noguchi paused, seemingly exhausted by his long speech. "If it becomes a police matter at all, Mr Shimizu's disappearance will, as the commander himself pointed out, be a matter for the Osaka force in the first instance. Mrs Shimizu may in any case not wish to report it at this stage: there is no obligation upon her to do so. All the same, and whatever he chooses to do in his private capacity about that, we must surely agree that it would be both improper and injudicious for the commander to be involved officially in investigating the possibility that his son-in-law might have been implicated in criminal activity.''

"Yes, yes, no need for a lecture, Hara. That's obvious." Kimura's testiness was worthy almost of the absent Otani himself. "I'm quite aware that all we might have here is a series of coincidences. Even so, it'll be a lot easier said than done to keep the Chief out of things. A lead is a lead, and if Mrs Otani really saw the pair of them together in Osaka last week I can't imagine him not following it up, whatever his daughter wants done about finding Shimizu. Meantime we shall have to do exactly the same thing. Can't just leave that side of things in the air.''

"Nobody's suggesting that." It was Noguchi again. "Want this whole mess cleared up, and quick. Plenty for all of us to do. Your job—the gaijin woman. Talk to her friends, contacts, that company she was with in Osaka for a while.''

He turned to stare at Hara. "As for you, use your imagination. Hang in close with East Central. DI Urabe's no fool, and he won't let you be too damn soft with those neighbours. Lean on them. Stands to reason somebody must have seen that great tall foreign bird around the place. It's well off the tourist beat and miles away from where the resident gaijin hang out. I'm going to stay with the Hinomaru angle. Got several bones to pick with friend Motoyama.''

Hara cleared his throat. "There's the matter of the district prosecutor," he said. "A preliminary report is already with him and he has already asked to be kept up to date on a daily basis. As Inspector Kimura has pointed out, the combination of the photograph and Mrs Otani's informal testimony indicates an avenue of investigation we're bound to explore. It's the sort of thing which would normally be passed on . . ." His voice trailed away as he became aware of the withering looks being directed at him by both Noguchi and Kimura.

It was Noguchi who broke the ensuing silence. "We may have had to upset the commander, son," he said glumly. "But I'm not having anybody in this headquarters blabbing to the prosecutor about his private affairs."

Chapter 8

OTANI HAD NOT ENJOYED THE REGULAR WEEKLY MEETing of the Kobe South Rotary Club at the New Port Hotel. Given his frustrated and anxious frame of mind he had not expected to, but in the circumstances it had been particularly trying to be stuck next to a visiting Rotarian from the Namba club in Osaka, an executive from Kansai Television. An oily man in every way, he combined pushiness with a nauseatingly dirty mind, and his whispered commentary on the guest speaker's earnest remarks about the role of women in contemporary Japanese politics was both ill-mannered and profoundly unfunny.

After well over ten years within the fold Otani was one of Kobe South's more senior members; not of course in the same league as the venerable Professor Masui who had retired from Osaka University at about the same time as Otani's own father vacated his chair in chemistry there, who had known him as a boy and still seemed to regard him as a promising young fellow with a bright future ahead of him. Masui was the club's grand old man, getting on for ninety, and there were several others whose dates of birth as given in the printed membership roster also harked back to the Meiji period. They were for the most part happy, garrulous old buffers, enjoying authority without responsibility and the effusive respect of the active members in their fifties and sixties who actually ran the club and who from time to time awkwardly suggested to Otani that he might consider serving on one of its committees.

He invariably declined, on the increasingly spurious grounds that he was precluded from taking on regular commitments of such a kind by the exigencies of his job which demanded his availability at all hours of the day and night. This had been true enough in former years, but these days he became involved only in such operational duties as he cared to. His real responsibilities as commander of the Hyogo force had much more to do with juggling the often conflicting priorities of the National Police Agency of which he and a handful of his most senior colleagues were officials, the prefectural government and its Public Safety Committee which employed everybody else in the force and was the channel for its funds, and the district prosecutor—currently a hard man given to making full use of the considerable independent investigative powers of his office.

What it all boiled down to was that Otani kept conventional office hours most of the time, and the Kobe South Rotary Club grandees knew this perfectly well. All the same they always looked relieved as they eagerly accepted his apologies and dropped the subject for another eighteen months or so. Men of their generation had much more ambiguous feelings about the police than their children and grandchildren, and with good reason. Even so, Otani had one or two cronies. The closest to him since the death of the man who had originally proposed him and engineered his election as a Rotarian was Fumio Iwai, who appeared at his elbow as he was leaving the big private dining room.

"Otani-san. Tried to catch your eye during the meeting, but you were too busy talking. You sick or something? Hot weather getting you down? You don't look very bright."

"Iwai-san! Good to see you. Yes, it's hot enough. But I'm fine, thanks."

"Time for a glass of iced tea before you go back to maintain law and order again?"

They were by then clear of the clusters of departing Rotarians, but Otani gave a quick glance round all the same to check that none were within earshot before he spoke again. "Yes. Good idea. I've . . . I've nothing urgent to attend to at the office. You certainly didn't see me talking in there, by the way. I was listening, with great reluctance. That man is disgusting. I wonder how on earth he got into the Namba club?"

Iwai grinned cheerily. "I would have warned you to steer clear of him if I'd arrived earlier. When I saw him favouring you with his company it occurred to me that you'd hardly take to the Slimy Monster from the Deep," he said. "That's what they call him in Kansai TV, after the cartoon character. No secretary there has ever been persuaded to work for him for longer than a month, and he even has to get his own coffee out of the dispenser machine. There's no accounting for those fellows over in Osaka. But then again, how on earth did I ever get into this club alongside all you respectable pillars of society?"

They were passing through the automatic glass doors at the main entrance to the hotel and Otani was spared the necessity to reply at once. "I have wondered, now and then," he admitted when they were outside in the thick heat and ambling slowly along the broad boulevard towards the innumerable coffee shops of the city centre. "I suppose it's because you're always so unobtrusively turned out. Besides, it's nice to be able to boast about our famous writer."

Iwai was several years younger than Otani, and had become a Rotarian while still features editor of the local newspaper, the *Kobe Shimbun*. Even then he had affected bow ties and other touches of eccentricity in dress and behaviour of the kind permitted to a journalist. Then a novel he had written had been a runaway best-seller, followed in rapid succession by two more. Iwai had hit upon the perfect formula, a heady mixture of daring eroticism, sophisticated humour and sly, perceptive social comment, and was sitting pretty. Two years earlier he had resigned from the newspaper and was developing a burgeoning side-line as a humorously subversive television pundit. The intricate unwritten laws of Japanese society accordingly authorised and indeed in a sense required much greater extravagance in his appearance, and month by month the bow ties became floppier and more exuberant, the fringe of hair round his bald dome longer and wilder, and the clothes ever more unorthodox.

Otani had read none of Iwai's books and was unaware that he appeared in one of them in the guise of a cabinet minister. Nor had he seen him on television very often, though Hanae was something of a fan. Their friendship dated from an occasion years before when Iwai had interviewed him for the paper, and official wariness on the one side and a degree of hostile aggressiveness on the other had within minutes given way to an extraordinary meeting of minds. From that day on they had enjoyed each other's company, and Iwai's dramatic rise to celebrity and riches made no difference to their carefully disrespectful attitude to each other.

"When's the next best-seller due to appear?" Otani enquired when they were settled in the first coffee bar Iwai pronounced suitable. He regarded iced tea as unnatural, and had ordered an ordinary cup of coffee.

"All in good time," Iwai said comfortably. "My chat shows keep me busy. And I've still got some research to do for the next book."

Otani understood the word "research" only in the purest academic context in which his father had used it, and produced a tired smile. "It's hard to see you sitting in a university library day after day for months on end," he said.

Iwai looked almost offended, then chuckled and sucked at the bright green plastic straw which protruded from between the lumps of ice which made up the greater part of the contents of the tall glass in front of him. "I'm surprised at you of all people, Otani-san. You're a trained observer yourself. How did you solve some of those famous cases of yours if not by noticing things about you and using your imagination? That's what I mean by research. Take a look round this place, for a start."

Otani did so. Apart from themselves and the waitress who had served them there were no more than half a dozen people in coffee bar Empress, which was on the pretentious side and

63

offered a choice of at least half a dozen different blends for the delectation of the connoisseur.

"Half of the customers are staring at you," he pointed out, turning back to Iwai. "And I expect the rest are only pretending not to. All probably wondering whether to ask for your autograph. I'm glad I'm not a television personality."

"You get used to it. It's power of a precarious kind, you know. And I love deflating some of the pompous characters I get on the show. Don't try to sidetrack me, Otani-san, or I'll invite you on to it and slice you up. The thing is, there's the makings of a short story in the manner and appearance of each and every one of the people in this coffee shop, and possibly a novel if you were to weave them together into a plot. That couple in the corner, for instance. Obviously both married, but not to each other. A commonplace situation, but who knows what emotions that private little smile of hers might disguise? She might even be meditating murder . . . they say it often turns out to be the quiet ones who go in for it, don't they, but you're the expert, of course."

Otani winced internally as Iwai rambled on, reflecting that if, as now seemed inescapable, his son-in-law had indeed been involved in a love affair with Marianna van Wijk it might have been what Iwai rightly called a commonplace situation at some stage, but was potentially tragic now that she was dead and Shimizu was missing. Otani was too seasoned an investigator to discount coincidence, but it was too much to hope that there was no connection between the two events.

Where was Shimizu? Presumably he knew of the foreign woman's death. Was he afraid of being compromised in some way as a result? Was he *responsible* for it in some way and on the run? Perhaps for the rest of his life? Or even— God forbid—dead himself too? A mood of black, self-pitying anger began to sour and obscure his thinking. How could he have been such a fool as to allow Noguchi and Hara to talk him so easily into excluding himself from the official investigation? When the well-being of his own daughter and of his grandson was at stake? It was ridiculous. He could not and would not stand on the sidelines hoping for the best, when his own close acquaintance with Shimizu over many years put him in by far the best position to assess and interpret such evidence as police methods might unearth.

". . . why on earth the unfortunate child decided to wear one Dayglo pink sock and one green one."

"I'm sorry, I didn't quite catch that," Otani said.

Iwai peered at him over the top of the half-glasses he affected and rattled the remains of the ice cubes in his glass with his straw. "Well, there's no need to look so cross about it," he said. "I was referring to a fat girl who just left. Perhaps seventeen or eighteen. Grossly overweight, probably glandular trouble, so why draw attention to her bottom by wearing clinging black trousers? It's of no consequence. I often talk to myself, Otani-san. And you're obviously distrait. Something on your mind?"

Otani nodded. "Yes, I am a bit preoccupied, I suppose. Not very good company, I'm afraid. Sorry. I'd better be getting back, anyway." Determination to be up and doing began to overcome the depression, and he was masterful in brushing aside Iwai's attempt to pay the bill.

"Don't think I'm being interfering," Iwai said as they went out into the dusty afternoon heat of the street again. "But if there's anything I can do . . . My phone rang this morning just as I'd got my face nicely lathered ready to shave," he went on blithely when Otani said nothing. "It was a nuisance, but of course I washed all the soap off again before I answered it, and thought at the time of that curious convention in the movies. You know, when the fellow's caught in the same situation and invariably wipes all the soap off on a towel. What a disgusting habit. Now you wouldn't do a thing like that, would you?"

His good humour was infectious, and Otani was able to manage a proper smile. "No, of course I wouldn't. And when my phone rings in the middle of the night I don't switch the light on before I answer it, either. They always do that in films, too. I can't think why, it gives you a headache and makes it impossible to get back to sleep again. It's perfectly possible to talk in the dark."

The two men became so absorbed in trivia that Otani too became oblivious to the stares of passers-by who recognised the well-publicised face of Furnio Iwai and assumed that his slightly less animated but still chatty friend was also something to do with television.

Chapter 9

THE YOUNG WOMAN BEHIND THE RECEPTION DESK AT THE offices of the Dejima Pharmaceutical Company apparently doubled as telephone switchboard operator, and Kimura decided at once that she must be new to both jobs. As he approached the desk she was stabbing repeatedly at one of the buttons on the contrivance at her side, muttering to herself while lights flashed and it emitted warbling, chirruping sounds. There were beads of perspiration on the bridge of her tiny nose and she managed only a brief, hunted glance in Kimura's direction before attacking the machine again. A few seconds later all the lights went out at once and the noises stopped.

"It seems to have broken down," Kimura said sympathetically.

"They'll have to get the engineer in again," she announced with grim satisfaction. "Third time this month." The receptionist was small but fierce-looking, and when she flung herself out of her chair and disappeared through the door behind her Kimura could see that the blue smock she wore was much too big for her. The smart company logo based on the roman letters DPC should presumably have settled in the region of her left breast but was in fact nearer her waist, and the sleeves were rolled back several times to bulk awkwardly round her little arms. The smock was so voluminous that it could have served as a maternity dress, and Kimura felt quite sorry for its wearer.

Not at all put out at having been deserted, he sized up his surroundings. Having looked the firm up in a directory of manufacturing companies before setting out, he knew already that Dejima Pharmaceuticals was not a long-established concern. The company's offices adjoined the "laboratories", as the manufacturing facility was pretentiously described in English as well as Japanese on a shared signboard beside the service road leading to the small industrial estate near the Yao district to the east of central Osaka. The same wording appeared in black on a brushed aluminium plaque at the side of the main entrance to the building, while a huge version of the red logo on the receptionist's smock was placed above the double doors, with the bulk of the building immediately behind two floors of offices.

The small lobby in which he was standing had a flimsy, almost temporary look to it. The flooring was of plain haircord carpeting the colour of dried blood, the walls covered with plastic veneer simulating walnut. A large framed photograph of a middle-aged man described as the founder and president of the company had pride of place on the wall facing the entrance, beside a narrow staircase leading to the upper floor. There were no other decorations except for a company calendar behind the reception desk. Its July photograph depicted a radiant girl in a swimsuit on a tropical beach of the kind advertised by travel agents. Wet sand clung to her smooth golden thighs, and she was drinking from a small bottle with a medicinal look to it and labelled "Gynojoy" in both roman script and the angular phonetic symbols reserved for foreign and therefore chic words. A good-looking young man in soft focus in the background was spreading a blanket on the silvery sand with a look of pleased anticipation on his face.

Kimura remembered seeing the product advertised in television commercials as being just the thing to make premenstrual tension a thing of the past, transforming miserable, irritable and sloppy "before" wives, girlfriends and office ladies into very different "afters": demurely contented and efficient home-makers, lively and responsive partners in romance or decorative, helpful and sexually aware colleagues as the case may be. It occurred to him that it might be a trying time of the month for the receptionist, and he was just concluding that if so her manner suggested that the company ought to supply the elixir routinely to female staff when she returned to her post.

"Typical! 'The equipment gave perfectly satisfactory service when Miss Tada used to operate it.' " Whether or not it represented an accurate impersonation, the fluting, hoity-toity accent she assumed made Kimura grin.

Encouraged, the receptionist continued to address him. "Ha! Miss Tada this, Miss Tada that, it makes you sick. Miss Tada never had to leave the board for two minutes to go to the loo. Oh dear no, she only used to do that in her own time. Evenings and weekends. And national holidays. Miss Tada never kept a book or magazine under the desk and took a little peep at it when nothing was happening. The famous Miss Tada was—"

Kimura was never to know more about this departed princess among receptionists, because her successor broke off in midsentence and rearranged her features into a sickly smile as they both heard a door open and close again upstairs, and a few seconds later the sound of footsteps on the stairs. The man who came into view was also wearing a blue company smock decorated with the logo, but his had short sleeves and a high collar with buttons to one side, and made him look like a fashionable if unusually colourful American dentist or surgeon. The lower half of his body was encased in grey trousers the fastidious Kimura would not have minded owning himself, and on his feet were highly polished and obviously expensive black casual shoes. He was of unremarkable height and build, and had a thick mop of hair done in a boyishly casual way although Kimura judged him to be at least in his late thirties. He had a moustache of the kind Kimura associated with militant western homosexuals: it covered his entire upper lip and curved slightly downwards round the extremities of his mouth, and Kimura disliked both the moustache and its owner on sight.

The newcomer paused on the stairs when he saw Kimura and surveyed him from above, while the receptionist simpered up at him. His leisurely scrutiny of the visitor seemingly completed to his satisfaction, he descended the last few stairs, made his way without a word to the rear of the reception desk and to the same door the mutinous young woman had earlier used. All at once looking petite rather than simply small, she sprang to open it for him and sagged in adoration as he went through, ignoring her completely.

"That," she hissed at Kimura conspiratorially when she had closed the door tenderly behind the odious man, "is Murata-*sensei*. Director of research. He's lovely." Then, without a pause, she assumed a brisk, businesslike manner. "What was it you wanted, then?" she demanded imperiously, almost as though it was she who had been kept waiting by Kimura, rather than the other way round.

He was taken by surprise, and hastily took out his wallet to select an appropriate name-card. He always carried a selection, mostly bearing his real name, but describing him variously as a freelance journalist, an encyclopaedia salesman or a public opinion pollster. He found that there were very few people who would decline to talk to him in the first or last of these fictitious capacities and often with the most startling freedom; while the role of encyclopaedia salesman was sometimes the best cover when he wanted to snoop round a whole neighbourhood. He also carried a supply of authentic cards as well as his police credentials, and though on the way to call at Dejima Pharmaceuticals he had flirted with the idea of assuming a bogus identity he now hesitated only briefly before handing over one of the genuine articles.

"My name's Kimura," he said. "Inspector, Hyogo Prefectural Police. I'd like to talk to whoever's in charge of personnel here."

The receptionist studied the card, nodding judiciously as though she had long been expecting a visit from the police. "I'm not surprised," she said darkly. "Mr Kano's reasonably sensible, you'd better see him. Wait a minute, I'll go and fetch him."

She disappeared again through the door behind her, returning quite soon in the wake of another man in a short overall smock similar to, but better fitting than the one which threatened to engulf her. Clearly, the office staff were not permitted the surgical style sported by Dr Murata.

In any case, Mr Kano's image was altogether different from that of his scientific colleague. He was a tall, gangling man who looked like a temperamentally cheery, enthusiastic soul, in spite of the worried look on his face as he introduced himself. Kimura felt sure that in his private life he pursued a demanding but essentially unintellectual hobby, like marathon running or leading a boy-scout troop. He was the soul of courtesy, and after no more than a moment or two of hesitation invited Kimura to follow him upstairs, loping athletically ahead of him and ushering him into a small room furnished only with a low table, a few easy-chairs upholstered in shiny black plastic, and a glass-fronted display case containing what had to be sample bottles and packages of the company's products.

Two other doors opened off the upstairs lobby, one bearing a sign indicating that it led to the president's office, the other obviously connecting to the other part of the building, which Kimura presumed was the domain of the supercilious Murata, the other scientific staff and those responsible for production. The soundproofing was excellent: Kimura had no idea how noisy the machinery needed for the mass-production and packaging of pharmaceutical products might be, but even though Kano had left the door of the little reception room open the tranquillity of the upper office floor was undisturbed, especially with the telephone switchboard out of commission.

Feeling that he had spent plenty of time already in getting this far, after the barest acceptable minimum exchange of courtesies Kimura came directly to the point. "Until recently you had a foreign lady temporarily attached to your company under the European Business Fellowship Scheme. A Miss Marianna van Wijk."

Kano nodded eagerly. "Yes, yes, a most . . . how shall I say, *impressive* lady. She speaks our language very well, and is so quick on the uptake! I may say that some of the staff here were a little bit nervous about her coming, but before very long we all treated her as one of the family. It was a happy coincidence that she was able to join us for the annual staff outing the Saturday before last. And now she's in . . . Fukuoka, isn't it? My word, we Japanese will have to look to our laurels when Europeans of Miss van Wijk's quality start competing seriously against us!"

Kano chuckled merrily at the thought, but when Kimura remained silent the troubled expression returned to his mobile face. He peered again at Kimura's card which he still had in his hand. "There is no . . . no *problem* about Miss van Wijk, is there, Inspector? We have heard nothing from her since she left us, but then I'm sure she must be very busy . . ."

Kimura had been wondering whether or not word of the woman's death had reached Dejima Pharmaceuticals, and Kano's innocent reaction to the mention of her name left him in two minds about enlightening him. His main purpose in visiting the firm at all was simply to form an impression of Marianna van Wijk as a person, and there was something to be said for letting Kano ramble on about her in ignorance about what had happened. On the other hand, the staff would be bound to find out sooner or later, and in Kimura's experience people often came out with unguarded, revealing remarks when something startling was sprung on them. He was therefore in something of a dilemma.

"We are just checking one or two details about her stay with you," he said carefully, having decided to string Kano along for at least a little longer. "If you wouldn't mind just confirming a few points?"

"Of course, Inspector. Our president is in Tokyo this week, but in his absence I'm sure he would wish me to cooperate on his behalf in every way with you in your, um, enquiries . . . that is, if there is, I mean, may I ask what—"

Kimura overrode his hesitations. "For instance, I'm not

quite clear how your company came to be included in Miss van Wijk's itinerary. I mean, did she ask to come here, or did Dejima Pharmaceuticals take the initiative in offering an attachment to one of the current group of Fellows?''

Kano waited some time before replying, and when he did it was in a way which made Kimura think he had probably been rash in taking him for a bit of a fool.

''You might perhaps have been better advised to address that question to the secretariat of the Federation of Economic Organisations in Tokyo, Inspector,'' he said stiffly. ''They administer the scheme. Not that our company is a member of Keidanren, of course, we are not nearly big enough. We are in membership of the Federation of Small and Medium-Sized Enterprises, which is in frequent friendly touch with Keidanren. So far as I know, Miss van Wijk requested—''

Kano abruptly broke off, stood up and went and closed the door, which he had been facing. Kimura had his back to it and saw nothing except the curious expression of mingled unease and distaste which flickered across Kano's face, but did hear a light footfall outside and the sound of another door being opened and closed again. The tall man returned to his seat and cleared his throat. ''Where was I? Yes. I was saying that my impression is that Miss van Wijk asked as part of her programme to observe a medium-sized, fairly recently established enterprise in operation. Our president is known to be eager to establish foreign links, possibly with a view to manufacturing under licence, and—''

''Mr Kano. I'm sorry to have to tell you that Miss van Wijk is dead.''

Kimura watched carefully as Kano raised a hand to his mouth in obvious horror; then slowly bowed his head and crossed himself, his lips moving silently. Although personally indifferent to religion, Kimura recognised and was surprised by the ritual movement of the hand, for he had hardly ever consciously met a Japanese Christian of any kind, much less a Catholic. There was no particular reason why he should, since he had read somewhere that only three in a hundred professed the Western faith, and only one of those owed obedience to Rome.

"I apologise for not having told you at once." He felt genuinely sorry, for there was now about Kano an air of stricken dignity, and he looked at Kimura in what could only be disappointment.

"Yes," Kano said. "It would perhaps have been kinder."

Kimura hurried on, more uncomfortable than ever. "I did have my reasons, Mr Kano. And I must now ask you to treat the information in strict confidence for the time being, because we are still looking into the rather puzzling circumstances in which Miss van Wijk died."

"When?"

"When did she die? Last Sunday."

"Can you tell me nothing more?"

"Not at present, I'm afraid. But I'm hoping that you can perhaps help us. I realise that she wasn't here for very long, but presumably some particular member of the staff was responsible for looking after her? Explaining your organisation and procedures and so forth?"

"Yes. I was." His eyes were moist, but Kano seemed to be regaining control of himself, and answered Kimura's subsequent questions with an air of distraction, but simply and straightforwardly.

"Where did she stay while she was with you?"

"With a British friend of hers. A young lady who teaches English at Osaka Women's University. Miss Penny Johnston is her name. She has an apartment not so very far away from here. Twenty minutes or so by the interurban train, I believe."

"I see."

"My wife and I would have been happy to offer her hospitality in our own home, and she was a welcome guest for supper with us on two occasions, but naturally Mariannasan—as she was happy for us to call her—must have felt more at ease staying in the home of a European friend of about her own age . . ." Kano paused and gazed unseeingly out of the window, seemingly lost in thought. Then he focussed again on Kimura. "You will of course tell Miss Penny Johnston this terrible news," he said in a manner which admitted no argument. "She has a right to know."

74

Kimura nodded. "She will be informed. From everything you've said so far, I gather you formed nothing but the best of impressions of, er, Marianna-san. And she got on well with other people here? Didn't seem worried, or preoccupied in any way . . . ?"

Twenty minutes later Kimura left the Dejima Pharmaceutical Company's premises in a profoundly thoughtful frame of mind. Afterwards he could not have said why, after ambling some twenty yards, he turned and looked back, but he was glad he did, because he caught a glimpse of the unmistakable face of Dr Murata gazing down at him from one of the upstairs windows, and then hurriedly being withdrawn from view.

Chapter 10

"**N**O. AKIRA ALWAYS SEEMED TO BE IN A GOOD MOOD in London. Even when he was frantically busy. We both enjoyed it so much there.' Akiko's eyes were closed, and although she had been sitting quietly and answering Hanae's questions more or less readily, she gave the impression of being adrift and rudderless on a sea of misery.

Hanae was bone-weary and rubbed her own eyes. The two of them had sat up talking into the small hours after her arrival at the house the previous evening, and after giving an unwontedly solemn Kazuo his breakfast and taking him to his kindergarten Hanae had cleaned the little house from top to bottom and dealt with three machine-loads of washing before persuading Akiko to walk to the shops with her. The sorry state of the household supplies worried Hanae almost as much as the disappearance of her son-in-law, and they spent a small fortune and had to take a taxi back with their booty before setting off again to fetch the little boy at lunch-time.

In the afternoon Hanae took Kazuo to the zoo to give Akiko the chance to lie down for a couple of hours, and all at once it was evening again, bathtime and bedtime for her grandson, and for Hanae a choice between going home to

Rokko, which she longed to do, and staying another night in an attempt to comfort her daughter. Much as she loved Akiko and agonised with her in her predicament, Hanae felt helplessly inadequate in the role of comforter, which was one she had hardly ever been called upon to assume even during her childhood. Akiko had been a grave, self-contained little girl capable of playing quietly on her own for hours on end and of a kind of bewildered resentment when disturbed. Looking back to those years, Hanae remembered too the intensity of Akiko's rapt concentration when taken as a treat to any kind of theatrical performance and the jealous privacy of her delight which made her consistently reluctant to talk about such experiences afterwards.

At the time the child's reactions baffled but amused Hanae, but in retrospect were another clue to the strength of the personality Akiko must have been nurturing and which expressed itself to alarming effect when she was a teenager. Alarming to her mother, anyway, though Otani had been awkwardly tender with their forthright daughter even when she harangued him at length about the evils of capitalism and his own share of guilt in accepting a salary to help sustain and police a corrupt social order. At such times Akiko had been in tears often enough, but they were tears of anger and frustration, not unhappiness. Her hot and extravagant emotions were seemingly channelled outwards; and her commitment to student activism seemed to armour her in invulnerable self-righteousness. Comfort was the last thing Hanae had been called upon to provide then or afterwards, when Akiko entered briefly into a period of torpor; what amounted to a chrysalid state from which she emerged quite soon afterwards as a composed, articulate young woman equipped with a wry sense of humour which must all the time have been lurking somewhere beneath all the earlier ideological turbulence.

Worried as Hanae had been about her recently, therefore, it was hard for her to come to grips with the idea that Akiko needed her emotional support, and still harder to know what to do about it. It was almost twenty-four hours since Hanae had told her what little she knew about Marianna van Wijk and the circumstances of her death: after Akiko had adamantly refused to report her husband's disappearance to the local police station, arguing wearily that it was quite bad enough that her father in his capacity as head of the neighbouring force knew about it, not to mention Akira's colleagues at the office. Akira had quite obviously decided to exclude her from his confidence, she went on, and there was no reason to suppose that he might be physically ill or the victim of an accident of some kind. In any case, in that unlikely event someone would inform her: Akira carried ample identification on him. No, he must have had some reason for behaving so inexplicably, and Akiko intended to try to salvage her own dignity by waiting as long as it proved necessary to find out what it was.

Hanae had no need to feign respect for her point of view, especially when Akiko went on to speak sadly but honestly of her growing sense of estrangement from Akira since their return from England, of his changed habits and manner towards her, and her own defensive reactions.

"It's probably something sordidly obvious like another woman." The ghost of a rueful smile. "Just like Akira if I'm right. He wouldn't be able to cope with a quiet bit on the side like millions of others. Without wrecking the family and his career, I mean. Too honest, damn him."

Akiko's own painful candour had made it impossible for Hanae to remain silent about the hypothesis of an affair, and that was when she spoke carefully but openly about what she had seen that afternoon near Osaka Station and what she now knew about the woman who had kissed Akira Shimizu. Akiko listened in total silence and when she had finished what she had to say Hanae marvelled at the impassivity of her expression. She was her father's daughter in so many ways, and had certainly inherited his poker face.

"Poor woman," Akiko had said eventually, but volunteered no more that night.

"No lies, no evasions. You know what you can expect if you try anything on." Shimizu hated Aoki's ugly, grating voice, hated his lumpy, misshapen head and coarse features, the

78

ever-visible stubble making the skin of his face look like dirty orange peel; and his spirit ached from the ingenious humiliations inflicted on him mercilessly since he had been in Aoki's power.

"You met her when? Where? The exact circumstances." Another stinging slap when he hesitated, the beginnings of a sob choking Shimizu momentarily, and then full recollection, a commingled flood of sounds, colours, tastes, smells and physical sensations.

Above all, the clean fragrance of her against the lushly decadent strawberry smell all around and the warm insistence of her fingers on his bare forearm that afternoon at Wimbledon the previous year.

"It's Mr Shimizu, isn't it? You were on the discussion panel at the London Business School last month."

"Yes. Yes, I was." Taken aback, but quite flattered to be recognised, especially by such a striking-looking woman.

"My name is Marianna van Wijk. From Holland. I wanted to try to speak to you after the discussion but there was no chance." Then an immediate switch from the English she spoke very much more fluently than he did into correct if curiously accented Japanese. "I hope to spend some time in Japan next year. There are scholarships for young managers, called European Business Fellowships."

"I have heard of the scheme," Shimizu said, courtesy fighting obligation as he spotted Mr Hasegawa waddling self-importantly back from the Gents, the long-peaked baseball cap he wore on his big head giving him something of the look of a cartoon character.

"I'm sorry, you're busy," she said as his eyes flickered back to her. "I do apologise. Perhaps—"

"What, at Wimbledon? Not at all. Please allow me to introduce you to my distinguished visitor. Hasegawa-san is one of the directors of my company." Relieved at being able to soften up the old bore by producing a Japanese-speaking western woman, even if she did tower over Hasegawa and was a couple of inches taller than himself. Their Centre Court tickets were on expenses, but Marianna had paid for her own which confined her to outer darkness and less newsworthy tennis. It didn't matter, though. Old Hasegawa was so charmed by her Amazonian good looks and friendly, unaffected manner that after quizzing her at length about her plans and ambitions he invited her to join the two of them for dinner that evening. Marianna reacted with neither coy hesitation nor overeagerness. She considered, nodded and accepted with composure, and took her leave of the two Japanese.

There was no reason why Shimizu should not have mentioned the encounter to Akiko when he went back to the flat in St. John's Wood to change after consigning an unusually affable Hasegawa to his hotel in the care of the hire-car chauffeur. She seldom expected and even more rarely wanted to accompany him when he was squiring visiting Japanese bigwigs round London, though she usually enjoyed hearing about their timidly wistful lustfulness when confronted late in the evening by the sight of the bare breasts of English showgirls and the wiles of the more soignée of the hostesses at the West End clubs dedicated to lightening the pockets of tired businessmen.

It would still have been perfectly possible for him to have told Akiko about Marianna at the end of the evening, and now he devoutly wished he had. It was innocent enough: extremely diverting for much of the time, watching Hasegawa preen himself and drink far too much while Marianna subtly flattered him over their lengthy dinner at the Café Royal. Oh, she had sung most beautifully for her expensive supper, winning Shimizu's admiration for her style and respect for her sensitive intelligence. By the time they eased a blissfully reeling Hasegawa into a taxi, took him back to the Savoy Hotel and made sure he had the right room key Shimizu felt a burgeoning sense of conspiratorial solidarity with her.

"Where to now?" The smile they exchanged was relaxed and amused, as though they had known each other for years: two sophisticated, ambitious people, adept at handling the Hasegawas of this world.

Marianna gave a little shake of the head.

"Don't worry about me, I can get the Underground. It isn't far to Camden Town."

"Well, *I'm* going to St John's Wood by taxi, at the company's expense. And Camden Town's on the way. Come on."

"I had nothing to feel guilty about," Shimizu protested to Aoki's implacably closed face. "We talked a bit in the taxi. Generalities. She'd obviously impressed Hasegawa, who could open all sorts of doors for her when she arrived here in Japan. We shook hands outside the door of the house where she shared a flat with another graduate student. Near the Zoo. Arranged to meet for lunch and a proper conversation the following week. I was home by half past eleven."

Aoki sneered. "No guilt. But not a word about this fascinating new lady friend to your wife. Just in case things might develop between you and this good-looking Dutchwoman. You fantasised about her over the next few days. Didn't you? Powerful white thighs wrapped round you. Big, generous breasts. A greedy wet mouth. That how it was?" Shimizu cringed as the assault went on. "If you weren't so pathetic I'd despise you. Just being helpful, eh? Informed advice to the young lady about how to get the most out of her year in Japan? International cooperation and understanding? Hypocritical waffle! If it had been a man, some ordinary-looking young man who'd asked you for help he'd have got—what? Half an hour in your office and then the brush-off if he was lucky. All right. This famous lunch. How far did you get with her that day?"

Chapter 11

THE DISTRICT PROSECUTOR LEANT BACK IN HIS CHAIR UNtil it creaked, and studied Otani over the top of his half-moon glasses. "We have occasionally taken somewhat different views of the cases we have discussed since I arrived here, Superintendent. That is only to be expected. I know that my predecessor in this post was inclined to—how shall I put it— involve himself in the active investigation of suspected criminal offences only rarely, while I see my responsibilities as entailing a more positive role."

"Prosecutor Ishiyama had confidence in me and my staff," Otani said. "We came to him when we were ourselves satisfied that we could lay before him irrefutable evidence justifying a prosecution; or in some cases with a recommendation against such action. I think it would be true to say that we never gave him cause to reconsider the basis of our working relationship, Mr Prosecutor."

He had known for months that he should try harder to get on with Hiroshi Akamatsu. There could be no doubt about the man's ability, after all. To achieve the rank of chief prosecutor and be placed in charge of one of the fifty District Public Prosecutor's Offices in the country at not much over forty was proof enough of that. Furthermore, Otani was well aware that Akamatsu was right in implying that the departed Ishiyama had been easy-going to a fault, little more than an affable rubber-stamp. His term of office had been most satisfactory from Otani's point of view, but now he must simply adjust to the new man's ways, for Akamatsu was not only perfectly entitled but indeed had a duty to involve himself and his staff in the investigation of crime, with the cooperation and assistance of the police.

"I do not doubt it for a moment, Superintendent. The many investigations which you and your able colleagues have brought to satisfactory conclusions over the years have won you a richly merited, national reputation. You are a formidable figure. Mr Ishiyama deferred to you not only because he rightly had great faith in your professionalism and judgment, but also because he found you intimidating. You look surprised, but I can assure you he told me so himself."

Akamatsu did not for his part look in the least intimidated. There was a quizzical expression on his long, horse face and when he had finished speaking he kept his mouth open, his lips concealing his teeth and forming a perfect "O", a black hole of what might have been silent laughter. It was one of his most irritating mannerisms, and Otani had more than once amused Hanae by demonstrating it to her.

"I am surprised. And disappointed, I must admit. I have always done my best to cooperate fully with the district prosecutor, and—"

"And I myself have no complaint whatsoever, Superintendent. On those occasions when I have as I mentioned felt obliged to register a difference of opinion you have been scrupulous to follow up my suggestions. But all that is rather by the way, because in the present case I cannot imagine that we could possibly disagree."

"On what?"

"On the crucial importance of maintaining the closest contact at every stage of the investigation of the circumstances surrounding the death of the foreign woman Marianna van Wijk. In this connection I take it that I may assume as a matter of course that any information which comes to light, however trivial, will be placed before me without delay."

"Of course I agree. All relevant information—"

"Forgive me for interrupting you, Superintendent, but I must be the judge of relevance. I—but I owe you an apology for having plunged into this slightly delicate subject before asking what I can do for you. It has been much in my mind, and on seeing you here I quite forgot that our meeting is taking place at your request."

The prosecutor's inviting smile was if anything rather more disagreeable than his black-hole expression, and Otani focussed on the bridge of Akamatsu's nose. It was a technique he often used: it enabled him to think fast and privately while the other person was convinced that he had his full attention.

"Yes. As a matter of fact, I asked to see you to let you know that I'm taking a few days" summer leave. I've cleared it in the usual way with the chairman of the prefectural public safety commission and notified the National Police Agency in Tokyo, of course. And needless to say, your office will continue to be fully briefed about current cases. So far as the Hinomaru Building affair is concerned, Inspector Noguchi will during my absence act as liaison officer—"

"Inspector *Noguchi*? Forgive me for saying this, but is he the ideal choice for . . . ?" Akamatsu's voice trailed off as he registered the bleak look on Otani's face. Otani let the silence stretch itself and then spoke coldly.

"You've rightly drawn attention to the responsibilities of your office, Mr Prosecutor. Those of mine include the deployment of my officers at my discretion. For your information, though, I will add that Inspector Noguchi is the most senior in rank among my headquarters staff inspectors. Furthermore, he is uniquely informed on all matters relating to organised crime in this prefecture, and is therefore taking the lead in investigating the Hinomaru Building arson case. Inspector Hara is working in close association with him, while Inspector Kimura is concentrating on the death of Marianna van Wijk."

Otani continued to glare at the prosecutor, pleased to have been given the chance to take the offensive. Akamatsu would be regretting his incautious remark about Ninja Noguchi, and wary about being too obviously inquisitive about Otani's personal plans.

"I see. May I ask how long you will be away, Superintendent?" The mouth was open again, the faintly amused look back in the hooded eyes.

"A week or so I expect, but I have no definite holiday plans and may be back sooner."

"Yes. Well, thank you so much for dropping in to let me know. I hope you will have a pleasant and relaxing break, and will look forward to seeing you on your return. Meantime I shall no doubt get to know Inspector Noguchi better."

"All right. Two more pages after you've had your bath," Noguchi said as the Haras' little daughter reluctantly clambered down from his lap in response to her mother's call. He put the book about the baby elephant carefully on top of the television set and reached for his beer. "A creep, that's what he is. But a clever creep," he said to Hara, who was nursing a weak whisky and water. "The commander must've been hardly out of the door before he was on to the governor's office to find out whether he'd asked for permission to leave the jurisdiction."

Hara's mouth twitched. "And how do you know that, Ninja?"

Noguchi shrugged massively. "Akamatsu keeps an eye on us. Only sensible for us to keep an eye on him. Prosecutors come and go. Staff down the line stay put. You want to find out what's going on in an office, pal up with the secretary or the switchboard girl."

"And has he?"

"Has he what?"

"Observed the rules for civil servants and sought permission to leave the prefecture."

"No. Time they got rid of that rule anyway. Treating us like a bunch of kids. No. He'll stay home, prowl about. And if he finds his son-in-law's at the other end of the country he won't go cap in hand to the governor to ask permission to go and fetch him back. Sachiko-chan sounds as if she's flooding your bathroom.''

Hara cocked an ear. "No. Just practising swimming."

"You all right, Hara? Look a bit down in the mouth. And since when do you drink whisky?"

Hara extracted himself from the inadequate easy-chair in which he had been sitting and stretched, his height and bulk making the tiny western-style room seem even smaller. Then he went to the open window and looked out at the identical block of flats across the forecourt. It was almost dark, and away to the west a flicker of lightning briefly emphasised the healthy purple of the cloud-bank which had gathered and settled over the city in the late afternoon.

"Won't be long till it breaks," Noguchi said. "Oh, hello, princess, finished already? All right, I'm coming. Two pages, right? Listen, if you hear something like thunder when you're in bed it'll only be my tummy rumbling . . ."

Hara was still at the window when Noguchi returned ten minutes later and tapped him on the shoulder. "Well?"

The younger man sighed heavily and turned to face him. "I made a few checks through central computer records this afternoon, Ninja. Including one on Akira Shimizu. He's on it, and cross-referenced to the Public Security Investigation Agency's restricted files at that. From what I can gather he was one of the most influential radical student leaders during the troubles in the sixties. It's the same man: no doubt about it.''

It was quiet in the room, and the rasping as Noguchi rubbed a hand over his stubbly chin and mouth was clearly audible. "Sit down, son," he said. "Finish your whisky. You won't need another."

He said nothing more until they were both back in their chairs. Then he shook his head slowly, his battered features softened into something like a smile. "You weren't to know, and I should have told you long ago. It's no secret, Hara. Just a case of once on a file, always on a file. Dare say the PSIA have got one on the commander's daughter too, come to that. He was a DI at the time. The Kobe University campus was in his manor. You're right. Shimizu was the brains behind a lot of the riots in these parts. And a long way further afield. The commander had to match wits with him. Arrested him more than once, then had to face anti-police demos led by his own daughter. She was a student there. One of Shimizu's, what's the word, groupies. To start with. Then it got serious between them, and she deputised for him whenever we had him out of circulation. Getting on for twenty years ago, Hara. All under the bridge. Shimizu's not the only one by a long chalk to have changed his mind and done well.''

Hara blinked incessantly throughout what for Noguchi had been an extraordinarily long speech, but otherwise remained perfectly still. Then, when Noguchi eventually reached for his beer glass and grimaced as he drained the flat remains, he took off his glasses and polished them with a paper tissue from an open box on the floor by his side. ''I see. It's a . . . surprising story, to say the least. To me. But as you point out, it all happened a long time ago, and you've adjusted to it completely. Like the superintendent himself, no doubt. Kimura knows all this too?''

''Sure. Like I said, it's no secret. Doesn't embarrass the commander in the least, he often has a joke about it over a drink.''

Exasperated, Hara leant forward, his fists clenched on his thighs. ''But good grief, Ninja, hasn't it occurred to any of you that not all of those old student factions from the sixties just faded away and died? All right, maybe ninety per cent—ninety-nine per cent if you like—of their membership was strictly temporary. Youngsters going through a romantic extremist phase; caught up in the mood of the moment. And I agree, some of the most prominent of the radical leaders put it all behind them within a very few years and went on to make their mark in ordinary life. I take your word for it that Shimizu was one of them. But we all know quite well that others—especially the so-called Central Core Faction—went underground. Surfaced again from time to time in the international terrorist context. And never quite shut down here, for that matter. Demos at the new Tokyo airport all through the seventies and early eighties and more recently uglier incidents. Bombs on railway lines, rockets aimed at the Imperial Palace during the last summit meeting—''

''All right, simmer down. Made your point. But if you're seriously suggesting that Shimizu's been playing a double game and managed to pull the wool over the commander's eyes all these years—''

''No, of course not, Ninja. New as I am here, I can see that the superintendent's much too astute a man for that. Given Shimizu's history, it's the other obvious possibility that bothers me.''

''Got any more beer in the fridge?''

Noguchi said nothing further until an exasperated Hara had hauled himself to his feet and disappeared into the miniature kitchen, been detained for a minute or two there in whispered conference by his wife and returned with a freshly opened bottle of Kirin beer and a plastic simulated lacquer bowl full of shredded dried squid.

Helping himself generously, Noguchi chewed thoughtfully, nodding slightly as he stared at Hara. ''Thinking of blackmail? Wouldn't work. Shimizu's never been ashamed of what he did that I know of.''

Hara gazed back with an earnestness which was almost painful. ''Not necessarily blackmail as such. Though even if Shimizu has been open about his activities in the sixties there might still be skeletons in his cupboard. Turn it round, though. Vengeance was what I had in mind. I haven't looked up the details, but there have been several well-known cases where one-time radicals like Shimizu have been beaten up, even murdered by former associates simply *because* they've changed their views. And how many other cases have there been that we don't know about? Shimizu must have had *some* reason for disappearing, for heaven's sake. It's at least conceivable that he might be on the run from his past. Or—''

''Or worse. Yeah. Should have thought of this sooner.''

Mrs Hara was suddenly in the room with a loaded tray. ''There isn't anything much to eat,'' she said shyly, the conventional phrase almost inaudible as her husband hurriedly got up and wrestled with the folding table. ''But please honour us by taking something.''

Chapter 12

SUDDENLY AWARE THAT THE TRAIN HAD STOPPED AT A station, Kimura was aghast to hear himself snore. He struggled back to full consciousness and peered out of the window in momentary panic; then relaxed again. Two more stops before he had to get off. He rubbed his eyes and looked around, irritated with himself. It was only nine in the evening, and he really shouldn't have dropped off like that. The interurban Hanshin Line was always busy, but at that time there were empty seats and Kimura noticed that his fellow passengers had given him a wide berth, presumably because they had taken him for a typical "salaryman", drunkenly bound for home and a long-suffering wife. He intercepted a censorious glance from a middle-aged lady wearing an unsuitable green hat and winked at her solemnly. Her silently outraged reaction made him feel better.

It had after all been a long and full day. After leaving Dejima Pharmaceuticals he had rung Osaka Women's University and discovered after being put through to a lady who sounded both vague and irascible that Marianna van Wijk's friend Penny Johnston was with a class but would probably be free half an hour later. Kimura had done the obvious and sensible thing and used the interval to go to the college by taxi, charm the first couple of students he came across on the campus and find out from them which building housed the staff of the English department. After that it was child's play to find the door with Penny Johnston's name on it, and with a minute or two to spare he was loitering elegantly in the corridor nearby.

His first reaction on sighting his quarry was that she must certainly have been told of her friend's death. Penny Johnston was tiny: diminutive even compared with the formidable receptionist at Dejima Pharmaceuticals, and painfully thin. Kimura judged that she had lost weight in recent weeks, for her clothes hung on her. A cloud of dark hair framed her pale, sad little face, and as she approached he could see purplish patches under her puffy eyes. The lecturers' names on the doors had included that of one other foreigner, a man, so this had to be Penny Johnston. And Miss Johnston had looked so utterly crushed that Kimura at once abandoned any thought of attempting to deceive her and introduced himself simply and sympathetically.

In retrospect Kimura thought it had probably helped the woman to sit with him in her cramped, book-lined little study and talk about Marianna, and especially at one point to have broken down completely and wept whole-heartedly. He was rather less sure whether the few things she told him that he hadn't already known would prove to be of much use, and even surer that Penny Johnston had been holding a good deal back out of misguided concern for Marianna's reputation. His tentative probing about the dead woman's circle of friends was met with what in less serious circumstances might have been charmingly unconvincing evasiveness.

He reached for the miniature tape-recorder he had during the past year or so taken to carrying on him, then checked himself. Better to play back the conversations with both Kano and Penny Johnston when he arrived home at his flat and then let a night's sleep give his brain time to digest the nuances, order the raw material and bring out any interesting features or suggest new lines of thought.

Emerging from his local station, Kimura looked up dubiously at the inky sky. With any luck the heavens would open some time overnight and wash some of the summer sultriness from the air, but on the whole he rather hoped the downpour would be deferred long enough for him to escape a soaking on the way home. With the possibility in mind he decided against filling the aching void in his stomach with spaghetti at Casa Sorrento near the station and went instead to the Shirayuki-tei or White Snow Pavilion on the ground floor of the building next door to the block of *manshon* apartments in which he lived. It hardly lived up to its elegant name, being a cheap and noisy Chinese restaurant, but it did serve the best steam-fried, garlicky stuffed, crescent-moon-shaped *gyoza* dumplings he had encountered in Kobe, cooked in full view of customers perched up at the narrow wooden counter by a young man of such singular beauty and sweetness of nature that Kimura had more than once idly reflected that if he ever were tempted to try homosexuality the *gyoza* cook would be the obvious person to approach first.

Having allayed his hunger with a first helping, washed it down with draught beer and ordered a second, Kimura sat contentedly enough amid the racket generated by the banging of woks, the shouting of waiters and cooks as customers' orders were passed on and acknowledged, and the occasional bursts of wild applause from the studio audience which were all that could be heard of a game show on the television set mounted high on a wall to one side.

It occurred to him that there was something to be said for being currently free from any sexual entanglement. Past experience suggested that his celibate state was unlikely to continue for more than a few weeks at most, but until some new woman acquaintance aroused his hunting instincts or he felt inclined to ring up one of the old flames whose addresses and telephone numbers filled several pages in his pocket diary it was nice to be able to eat as much garlic as he liked. The thought led him back to Penny Johnston, who had definitely not set his sensitive sexual antennae quivering.

She was, he thought, probably a few years younger than Marianna van Wijk: about twenty-eight or nine, but as skinny as a prepubescent twelve-year-old. He supposed that with some make-up on she might have a certain elfin charm, but deathly pale and miserable as she had been that afternoon in the aftermath of the tragedy she gave out nothing but a sense of passive vulnerability.

Kimura had been unsurprised to be told that Penny had heard the news of Marianna's death—"overcome by fumes in a burning building"—through a phone call from a friend at the office of the EC Delegation in Tokyo. He had himself been in touch with an official there to discuss practicalities like notifying the family, funeral arrangements and the disposal of belongings and been told that everything would be dealt with jointly by the EC Delegation staff and consular officers at the Netherlands Embassy.

During his conversation with Miss Johnston she said nothing to indicate that she had any idea of the use to which the Hinomaru Building was normally put, or of the kind of people who occupied it. She explained that she had known Marianna for several years. They met in London soon after the Dutch girl began her MBA course at the London Business School. Marianna had sought out people with a common interest in things Japanese, and begun to attend the regular meetings of an informal organisation of young British graduates who had all worked for a year or two as teaching assistants in Japan under a scheme sponsored by the Japanese government. Penny was a member, having already spent two years teaching English at a high school in the Tokyo area. Unable to find the right sort of job after returning to England she was filling in time by working as a guide-interpreter for the London branch of a Japanese tourist agency while trying with the aid of her contacts there to find longer-term academic work in Japan.

The offer to Penny of the lectureship at Osaka Women's University had come halfway through Marianna's time in London, and by then the two women had become good friends. They kept in touch by letter after Penny returned to Japan in time for the start of the academic year the following April, and when in due course Marianna arrived there to take up her fellowship it was the most natural thing in the world for Penny to offer her friend a bed whenever she came to Osaka to see her while she was undergoing intensive language training, and then for a period of six weeks when her study-attachment itinerary brought her to the area. Kimura knew that this sort of casually generous hospitality was routinely offered and accepted by young foreigners living in Japan, who, as he was also well aware, maintained a highly efficient communication network among themselves. As he just managed to find room for the last of his second helping of *gyoza* he made a mental note to try to find out what if any rumours were circulating among other young Europeans who must have met her about Marianna's death. Penny Johnston had not mentioned any.

Kimura burped discreetly as he made his farewells to the handsome cook, clambered down from his stool and took his bill to the girl at the cash desk near the door. The storm had broken and rain was bucketing down outside the restaurant, but by edging along close to the side of the building Kimura managed to stay reasonably dry. All the same, as soon as he was inside his flat he took his trousers off, patted the damp bottoms of the legs back into shape and put them in a clamp before looking through his mail. Nothing in it was of any interest, and he stripped off the rest of his clothes, took a shower and pottered about getting ready for bed. An early night wouldn't come amiss.

So Marianna and Penny had been friends of some years' standing, and there must be several other people like Penny up and down the country with whom Marianna had kept in touch and very possibly stayed with during her travels in Japan. It was understandable that Penny should grieve for her friend, but she could hardly have lost so much weight in the few days since Marianna's death, to the extent that her clothes were visibly too big for her? Could the relationship between the two women have been one of more than straightforward friendship? Of love, perhaps, so that Penny had been cast into despairing jealousy some time earlier, on learning that Marianna was pregnant? Why had Penny not been more curious about the circumstances of Marianna's death?

Whether or not she knew Marianna was pregnant Penny must surely have known about her relationship with Akira Shimizu: Kimura was well aware that women friends open their hearts to each other far more readily and completely than men do. Then there was the furtive interest shown in him by the supercilious Dr Murata at Dejima Pharmaceuticals. What was that all about? Kimura sighed as he took his jacket from the chairback over which he had draped it, removed the little tape-recorder from the inside pocket and arranged the jacket lovingly on a hanger.

Then he switched off the lights, went through to his austerely furnished bedroom with the tape-recorder in his hand and slid into bed. One of the amenities provided by the property developers which justified their describing Kimura's two-room flat and the others in the block as "sophisticated luxury accommodation for the discerning" was central air-conditioning, and the dry coolness of the bedclothes was indeed welcome after the stickiness of the outside world.

He switched on the tape-recorder, ran the tape back and then lay flat on his back in the dark supporting his head on his hands, listening to his own voice and that of Kano, the personnel man at Dejima Pharmaceuticals. The quality of the recording was poor, but adequate for the purpose, and he played the conversation back twice before moving on to the second one, with Penny Johnston. Kimura had heard less than half of it when the telephone in his living room shrilled out. With a muttered curse he switched the little gadget off and blundered through the door to answer it, stubbing his toes against a chair-leg in the dark.

"*Moshi-moshi?* Yes. Kimura speaking. Oh, it's you, Chief. Good evening. No, not at all. Quite alone, I assure you. I was working on some notes as a matter of fact. What? No, nothing I could put my finger on as yet, but . . . yes, of course, hang on a minute while I get a bit of paper . . . Right, I've got that. I presume there's no word from your son-in-law, then? You've been doing what? Oh. Well, I hope you enjoyed it, but I don't quite understand . . . Yes, of course I will, Chief, if you really think . . . yes, yes, I won't forget to tell them. Yes, the personnel man at Dejima Pharmaceuticals, and then on to Osaka Women's University to talk to the English girl she was staying with. Yes, obviously very bright, but completely shattered by what's happened, and hardly in a state to cope with too many questions at the moment. Well, quite honestly, Chief, I've hardly had time to sort out my thoughts yet. Can I sleep on it and get back to you tomorrow? Oh. I see. Well, if you say so of course, but . . .''

It was nearly another half an hour before Kimura was able to put the phone down, and then sleep eluded him for a long time.

Chapter 13

"**Y**ES, OF COURSE I WANT TO HELP THE SUPERINTEN-
dent in any way I can, gentlemen. But it seems to me that
we can best do that by concentrating on what is clearly and
indisputably our job. If the Osaka force get to hear about
these interviews you've been conducting over there—or the
district prosecutor for that matter—it would mean trouble for
him as well as for you."

"Oh, come on, Hara! Do you seriously imagine those lads
never slip over to our side of the line and prod around without
letting us know? They're not such sensitive plants as all that.
Anyway, nobody's asking *you* to bend the rules. The Chief's
on duly authorised leave, and if he cares to give me a ring at
home to talk about this and that and just happens to mention
something relevant to a current case, well, that's not the
prosecutor's business."

Hara shook his head worriedly, but before he could say
anything else Noguchi stirred in his chair, with the usual
result that his colleagues turned to him attentively. "He told
you he'd been watching TV, did he? And said you should let
me know?"

Kimura nodded. "Yes. It struck me at the time as being a
bit odd."

"What time was it he rang you?"

"Not all that late. About ten-thirty. Eleven maybe. Hang on, he has a paper brought here every day, doesn't he? I'll bet nobody thought to stop it while he's away."

As he spoke, Kimura hauled himself to his feet and went over to the side-table by the wall near Otani's desk. He was right. There beside a stack of old circulars from the National Police Agency, an ancient dictionary and a Japanese translation of *Monsieur Monde Vanishes* by Georges Simenon was a neat pile of newspapers with that day's *Mainichi Shimbun* on top. Kimura checked the date on the one underneath it, removed it and took it back with him to his chair.

Noguchi paid no attention to him as he grunted, rubbed his nose and looked at Hara. "You're going along with Urabe to talk to this old girl he's dug up, are you?"

"Yes. Later this morning. We'll show her some photographs."

"Took her time speaking up, didn't she?"

Hara shrugged. "I'm not particularly optimistic."

"Wait till you hear what she has to say. Myself, I'm having another sniff round Motoyama. As for you, Kimura, you'd better have a word with one of your spook friends at the PSIA. Hara's right. You and I might have got careless about Shimizu's background."

Kimura had opened the newspaper at the television programme page but not yet studied it. He pulled a face. "I don't know about that. I'd rather go a bit deeper into the set-up at Dejima Pharmaceuticals. Talk to the toffee-nosed scientist I told you about. Murata. Even if we haven't done anything about Shimizu yet, I can't believe it hasn't occurred to the Chief to think about that side of things."

"No doubt he has," Hara said. "But he's hardly in a position to take it up through official channels. You can."

"No I can't. Not until his wife formally reports him missing—to the *Osaka* police, let me remind you. In view of the family connection they might very well consult us if and when she does do that, but . . ."

"Be your age, Kimura. You're artful enough to find out

98

without making too many waves whether his PSIA file's been on anybody's desk lately. Bet it has.''

Kimura sighed. ''All right, Ninja, I'll try. But I still think you and Hara are off beam. Yes, I grant you there's clearly some sort of link between Shimizu and the Dutchwoman. And that his vanishing has something to do with her death. But I'm hanged if I can see any pointer to a political dimension—''

''Except what the commander told you on the phone last night.''

Kimura assumed an expression of long-suffering patience. ''All he said, Ninja, was that his daughter had been to see Shimizu's boss, the executive director of his company. And that he didn't seem to be particularly bothered by the disappearance of one of his liveliest managers, even though he couldn't offer any explanation of where her husband might be except that he'd been overworking and might have gone off quietly somewhere for a few days' peace and quiet on his own. Told her not to worry too much; and rather pooh-poohed the idea of reporting Shimizu as a missing person. Could mean anything or nothing.''

Hara coughed delicately. ''The, er, executive director. He presumably knows about Shimizu's past?''

Kimura shrugged. ''Presumably, but I really couldn't say. The Chief said that when Mrs Shimizu told him about the conversation he agreed with her in thinking that the director's attitude was a bit odd, but as I see it what else would a man in that position say when confronted by a distraught wife? Try to calm her down, get her out of his hair, and hope for the best that Shimizu will turn up in a day or two. It's what I'd do myself, probably.''

Noguchi was sitting up straight in his chair for the first time since they had gathered in Otani's office, both eyes fully open. ''Kimura. How many times have you met Shimizu?''

Kimura scratched the top of his head. ''Not very often. I went to their flat during that business over the netsuke, I remember. And I've seen him once or twice at the Otanis' house. I've never had anything amounting to a proper conversation with him, though.''

"Do you think he might have killed the gaijin woman?"

"The Chief's son-in-law? Good heavens, no. Entirely possible that he was screwing her, mind you. Lively-minded sort of man—"

"Save it. Right. I've met him a good many times. I don't see him as a killer in any circumstances, either. Hara here's never set eyes on the man. So he's not prejudiced. Shimizu's an obvious suspect from his point of view. Right, Hara?"

Hara surprised Kimura by shaking his head firmly. "Certainly not," he said primly. "There is nothing in the postmortem report, nor as yet any other physical evidence to suggest that Marianna van Wijk was murdered with intent by anyone. We have a prima facie case of death by misadventure. We have evidence of arson, and assuming that the guilty parties can be identified they will probably face a further charge of manslaughter. I fail to see how we can even hypothesise murder unless it can be shown that Marianna van Wijk was deliberately lured into the building by somebody who knew it was about to go up in flames. Even if he was responsible for her pregnancy, the disappearance of the superintendent's son-in-law suggests to me nothing—in that context—except that he should be found as quickly as possible and questioned."

Kimura pretended to applaud. "Well said! And how do you propose to set about that, pray?"

Hara ignored the jibe. "As I said to Inspector Noguchi yesterday evening, what I now know about Shimizu's former associations—and what the rest of you have known all along— makes me wonder whether he might have been abducted rather than gone into hiding voluntarily. That's why I think we ought to put out discreet feelers to the PSIA."

"Been thinking about that," Noguchi put in. "Not Middle Core Faction style with ex-comrades they decide have turned traitor. Nor Red Army. To deal with them on the quiet, I mean. No. They go for maximum publicity."

Hara chewed at his lower lip. "I hope you're right, of course," he said. "But time will tell. It's only been a few days, after all."

Kimura had finally turned his attention to the details of the previous evening's television programmes, and suddenly looked up. "The old fox! I'll swear he's telepathic. And it nearly slipped my mind this morning. Listen. The only remotely relevant programme at that time last night was a documentary special about new trends in drug abuse. On the very day a clever pharmacologist found out from the receptionist who I was and decided to take an interest in me!"

"I can read you like a book, you worm," Aoki said. "I know when you're lying, and I know when you're holding back."

Shimizu hung his head and surreptitiously wiped the flecks of Aoki's spittle from his cheek.

Then Aoki spoke more quietly, and his manner was all at once no longer crudely bullying but reasonable, almost plaintive. "Surely you'd rather tell me here, in private? You didn't enjoy the last session in front of the others, did you? Having to admit to them how the woman intrigued you, then fascinated you, then obsessed you? You, the one-time leader that everybody looked up to, practically worshipped? They're your judges now. You've accepted that much at last. People you would have despised not so very many years ago. But they don't have to hear every sordid detail. I do."

During the protracted nightmare of the past few days there had been moments when Shimizu felt the black imminence of total defeat, a despairing conviction that there was no point in resisting any more. Yet whenever the pit yawned in front of him Aoki seemed to come out with something which made him angry. Increasingly Shimizu reached out for that anger and grasped it as something precious, a link with sanity, with the world of ordinary people passing to and fro so near the place of his confinement, with his wife Akiko and his son Kazuo. He raised his head slowly and stared up at Aoki.

"You don't know what you're talking about," he said, fighting to keep the quaver out of his voice. He felt physically weak: he had been deprived of sleep and the food they gave him from time to time was as disgusting as it was pathetically inadequate, a bowl no more than half filled with rice, cold, slimy vegetables and weak but bitter green tea of the cheapest kind. "I have no regrets. Neither you nor the others will ever understand that."

How could they begin to imagine the colour and excitement of his affair with Marianna? Or its inevitability after their first few meetings in London: meetings of mind and spirit increasingly touched with the magic of mutually acknowledged sexual attraction? Which of them had made the first move? Shimizu could no longer remember, but even in his present misery he knew that there had been a kind of holy privacy but no furtiveness about the first time on a sunlit afternoon in the Camden Town flat. He had felt touched with wondering glory afterwards and in the ensuing weeks; yet it had not seemed at the time as though he were cheating Akiko of anything. On the contrary, it was as though his exultant happiness filled him with loving tolerance, enriching rather than souring his relationship with her.

"It *is* possible," he went on, not so much to Aoki as to himself. "There can be sexual relationships characterised by mutual desire without possessiveness, combining friendship with respect."

"And spiced with betrayal," Aoki said. "And don't give me any crap about being entitled to 'personal fulfilment'. We're not interested in that here. The woman arrived in Japan several months before you got back and took up bourgeois residence in Senri New Town. So you parted in London, no doubt with the *Liebestod* from *Tristan und Isolde* on the record player. Delicious self-indulgence, and you cried half the way home to St John's Wood. During the rest of the journey you thanked your lucky stars it had ended so tidily, with your wife none the wiser. What you didn't bargain for was that your sexy Amazon wrestling partner didn't take up with anybody else when she arrived in Tokyo, and was more or less waiting on your doorstep when you got back here, all ready and eager for Round Two."

"I *will* kill you, Aoki. Somehow, somewhere I'll have my chance."

"Oh my, you do scare me. Still so sorry for yourself, aren't you? Still thinking in terms of 'pride', 'dignity', 'self-respect' and all the rest of the pretentious clothes you try to wrap round your shoddy little self-consciousness.''

"*It wasn't like that, damn you!* The affair *was* over. She knew it, I knew it. But we were friends. Glad to see each other again. And then, before long, she needed not only advice but help. Urgent help. And she had only me to turn to.''

Even as he spoke Shimizu saw in his mind's eye a vivid picture of himself sitting at his desk taking the telephone call that was to turn his life upside down. Oddly compounded of coarse vulgarities and subtle insights as they were, Aoki's insults struck home every time. It was true that he had been apprehensive about Marianna by the time he returned to Japan with Akiko and the child. The sweet agony of their parting in London had been bearable only on the understanding that they would meet again after a few months, but they exchanged no letters and on arriving back in Osaka Shimizu had hesitated about getting in touch with Marianna again.

Then a visit to Tokyo while she was still in full-time language training there had led to an impulsive telephone call and a meeting in a coffee bar. He was clumsy and awkward, she friendly but at first little more than polite. Then the—yes, he had to admit it—the relief when she abruptly put down her cup with a twisted, heartbreaking little smile, touched his hand and said, "Don't worry, Akira. I know everything's different here. It will be lovely just to see you sometimes, but . . .''

"You don't expect me to believe that, do you? When you've already admitted that as soon as you were in touch again she started making excuses to come to Osaka on visits? And pulled strings to get an attachment to a company down here? Just how long did this nobly platonic arrangement last . . . before you decided you might just as well take what was on offer again?''

"You've a foul mind, Aoki. You soil and degrade everything you mention. You know quite well that by the time I saw her in Tokyo Marianna had already been to Osaka several times to visit a friend. A *woman* friend. And that the

103

attachment to Dejima Pharmaceuticals had already been arranged.''

''Enter the famous Miss Penny Johnston and her lover the talented and enterprising Dr Murata. Yes. Your judges and I need to be very clear about all that, *Comrade* Shimizu.''

''I've told you everything I know,'' Shimizu muttered dully, the sustaining surge of his anger spent.

''You lie. Not about everything, perhaps. I accept that the English girl was hired to hold an English conversation class at Dejima Pharmaceuticals once a week soon after she started at Osaka Women's University. Nothing special there; all college teachers moonlight. But you haven't explained how she came to meet the oh-so-internationally-minded head of the company in the first place.''

''How the hell should I know? It's of no importance.''

''Except that it had important consequences from our point of view, comrade. First, Murata rather surprisingly joined the conversation class. Then, and not in the least surprisingly in view of what you've said of him so far, he very soon got into Miss Penny Johnston's pretty little Marks and Spencer pants. It *is* Marks and Spencer, isn't it? It's a long time since I was in London . . . You aren't amused, I see. You find me crude. Vulgar.

''Very well, I will turn to the other, even more important consequence. The English girl became something of a mascot so far as the Dejima boss was concerned. Showed that his company was keeping up with the times. I dare say he even sat in occasionally on a conversation class himself, to set his minions a good example. Had little chats with her in his office about international understanding . . . oh, no hanky-panky there, of course. Our little English rose had her hands full—so to speak—coping with the randy Dr Murata. But on one occasion she did just happen to mention to the boss that a Dutch friend of hers was due to arrive in Japan shortly on a business study fellowship, and perhaps suggested that it might be nice for one of her attachments to be to Dejima Pharmaceuticals.''

''Perhaps.''

Aoki stood up, took a few steps towards the door and then

suddenly wheeled round, came back to the kneeling Shimizu and grabbed the front of the thin, patched blue yukata which was all they had given him to wear after taking his clothes away from him. He was a powerful man and without any apparent effort dragged Shimizu to a half-upright position, shook him briefly like a rag doll and then flung him back to the unyielding bare planks of the floor.

"Your attitude continues to be entirely unsatisfactory," he said then in an unexpectedly thoughtful, almost gentle manner as he loomed over the whimpering man. "I may have to contemplate alternative methods. There are several open to us here. Think about it, my friend. For one way or another, if justice is to be done you must hold nothing back, but confess everything . . . with joy."

Chapter 14

"I DON'T KNOW WHAT SHE'S GOT A BEE IN HER BONNET about this time, straight, but you shouldn't pay attention to her," the sharp-nosed woman said, and worked her pursed lips as though dealing with a pickled plum, something which nobody could possibly enjoy at the time but often seems in retrospect to have been worthwhile. "She imagines things. You ask the rozzers at the police box down the road. I've only got to pop out of the house for a bit of shopping and she's round there as quick as lightning telling them the tale that I'm trying to poison her or pinch her bit of savings."

"Yes, well, old people have their funny little ways. But then none of us are getting any younger," Inspector Urabe said comfortably. "My wife often says I'll be forgetting my own name one of these days."

"I don't see why you can't ask her whatever it is you want to know in front of me. All this hole-in-the-corner nonsense. Keeping her sitting out there in a car with that fat man and a bit of a girl. Poor old soul must be frightened to death. I shall have my hands full after you all push off, I don't mind telling you."

"Well now, Missis, it wasn't our idea to begin with, was it? I did ask if you'd be good enough to go out for half an hour and leave us to have a quiet word with the old lady, but you wouldn't have it, would you? Anyway, she jumped at the idea of going out to the car, called you something rather rude when you tried to talk her out of it, as I recall. So never you mind. My colleague Inspector Hara wouldn't hurt a fly, and the young lady with him's a very experienced police officer. Got a way with her, she has, and she'll make sure your mother-in-law doesn't get overtired or upset. Suits me, I must say. I'm quite enjoying our little chat.''

Urabe sipped from his cup of green tea, wiped his mouth with the back of his hand, nodded his head appreciatively and wiggled his toes. "Good to get your boots off once in a while during the day and feel tatami under your feet," he said. "You've got a lovely place here, Missis. And you keep it nice. Be glad to have your husband home again, though, I expect. In time for New Year, that right?''

The woman folded her arms across her scrawny chest and glared down at the inspector, incongruous in full uniform, pistol at his belt, but lacking his boots and with a hole in one of his socks.

"Whatever he may have done or not done to deserve it, he's doing his time quietly and not giving any trouble. There's no need for you to be sarky.''

"Me? Sarky? Not my style, Missis. Live and let live, that's my motto. All I said was you've got a nice place here.''

Though its exterior was drab enough, the little house was indeed well furnished, and clean and neat inside. The large television set looked almost new and there was an expensive video recorder linked to it. From where he was sitting Urabe could see into the kitchen area, which boasted a fair-sized fridge-freezer and a microwave oven, also new-looking. He smiled blandly at the woman as he caught her eye again. "All paid for too, I'll be bound. Nice to see Mr Motoyama's got a conscience.''

"And what's that supposed to mean?''

"Now, now. 'Whatever he may have done or not done to deserve it'. That's what you said, but you know as well as I do that your old man practically took us by the hand and showed us where and how he stashed away those shooters.

Why, if he hadn't been so forthcoming and anxious to stress in writing that it was a purely personal project we might have been obliged to arrange for Mr Motoyama himself to go down, mightn't we? Because to tell you the truth we were quite surprised when your old man spoke up. One or two of my people were actually cynical enough to suggest that he'd been chosen to take the rap on Mr M's behalf, but you can't quibble over a spontaneous confession from a veteran gangster, can you? I must admit I'm beginning to wonder if there was some mistake somewhere, though. If there was I'm sure Mr Motoyama will make it up to your husband in due course. Meantime it's nice to see that he's making sure you don't want for any little comforts.''

"I don't have to put up with this kind of talk. It's bad enough having a police car parked outside a respectable house without you coming in making insinuations. Why don't you go and make a nuisance of yourself somewhere else?''

Urabe's mouth twitched. "I wouldn't worry too much about the neighbours if I were you. Last few days there's been police cars parked outside enough homes in this area. Not the first time somebody's been here to ask you a few questions for that matter, is it?'' He unbuttoned one of the pockets of his tunic, took out a folded sheet of paper and then read aloud from it, assuming a mock-formal tone. " 'Mrs Okada stated that she had never heard of the Hinomaru Building. Reminded of the fact that it was situated approximately one hundred and fifty metres from and partly in view of the house in which she had lived for at least ten years she agreed that she must have passed it on numerous occasions, but said that she had never noticed it particularly. She was not aware that the building had been destroyed by fire within the past twenty-four hours. She had heard no fire appliances in the vicinity at any time on Sunday: she must have been watching television at the time.' Ah well, never mind. Most of your neighbours made very similar statements when we came calling.'' He sighed and refolded the paper carefully before tucking it away again.

"Trouble is, this business has kept us all so busy that we've had to bring in a lot of extra help. The patrolman who spoke to you is from a different division. Had no idea that he was addressing the grass widow of the unselfish Mr Okada. Wasn't till this morning that somebody did some cross-checking and pointed out that the Mrs Okada who wanted a word with us is that gentleman's mum. So I'm not surprised you're a bit on edge, wondering what on earth she's telling my colleagues out there. Why don't you take the weight off your feet and have a cup of tea yourself?''

Irritation, distaste and wary apprehensiveness warred for supremacy in Mrs Okada's manner, but she did reach for a flat *zabuton* cushion from the top of a small pile of them in the corner, drop it on to the tatami matting and sink to her knees at a safe distance from where Inspector Urabe was sitting cross-legged.

"That's better," he said. "Shouldn't think they'll be long out there, but there's one or two things I'd like to ask. And try not to worry. None of this'll get back to Motoyama, I promise you.''

Mrs Okada made a derisive sound, half laugh, half snort. "Tell me another," she said.

"I mean it, Missis. Live and let live, that's what I said before. And until a few years ago it didn't work out too badly so far as the Hinomaru lot were concerned. Motoyama's a nasty bit of work, but he used to play by the rules, more or less. And I know your old man's not much of a villain really.''

"He's loyal.''

Urabe raised a hand pacifically. "I know that. And very likely he will be properly taken care of when he gets out, just like you're being taken care of while he's inside. We understand each other, and I can live with this kind of situation. Been doing it long enough, after all.'' He rubbed his nose. "We're not fools, you know. And as far as the gangs are concerned, better the devil you know than the devil you don't. As long as Motoyama and his Hinomaru outfit stuck to their local everyday rackets we all knew where we were. I didn't go out of my way to upset the apple-cart. But ever since the old syndicate boss died things have been in a right mess, as you very well know. The Motoyamas of this world don't

109

know who's really in charge at the top. Most of them are simply hanging on, trying to cover their bets and hoping that when the dust finally does settle they'll be allowed to keep their little slices of the action. Some of them are getting a bit too big for their britches, though. Entertaining ideas above their station. Greedy. And Motoyama's one of them.''

"I don't bother my head with none of that." The look in Mrs Okada's bright little black eyes belied her words.

"Ah. Maybe you should take an interest. Whatever happens I reckon somebody'll find a slot for a useful man like your husband. Loyal, like you said. Only I have a feeling it won't be Motoyama, see? Because he's moved out of his proper league. And he's going to be clobbered for it. By the big boys. And by me if I get the chance." Urabe's manner had abruptly hardened. "Right. That's enough messing about. The old lady knows something about that fire. Has she said anything to you?"

The woman's hands were restless on her lap and her mouth worked again, but the lengthening silence was broken by the rattle of the sliding front door being opened, and Urabe turned as he heard Hara's schoolmasterly voice. "Are you there, Inspector Urabe?"

"In here, Hara. No, hang on a minute, don't bother to take your boots off." Urabe scrambled to his feet and looked down at Mrs Okada. "Think it over, Missis. I'll be back."

"Well done, Ninja. *Very* well done."

"Nothing to do with me. Hara and Urabe between them got it out of her. Dare say young Junko-san did her bit too."

"Yes, I'm sure she did. She's an extremely able detective." Otani made an effort to smile. "You say the old lady wanted to sell the information? How much did she ask?"

"Got to hand it to her for cheek. Started off by saying she wouldn't say a word till they promised to let her son out of jail. Then when she saw that wouldn't wash she said she'd settle for fifty thou to be going on with. Not a bad price. Urabe reckons Motoyama must be stumping up about that much every week to keep the Okadas going so comfortably. There's a teenage girl at high school. Anyway, Hara hummed

110

and hawed and said he'd see what could be done. Myself, I'm inclined to give the old girl her money. You look a bit rough.'' Noguchi stared at Otani with concern written all over his battered face.

''It's a worry being at arm's length from everything, but I'm feeling a lot brighter now, thanks to you . . . and the others, of course.'' Otani pushed away the thick white plate with the remains of his curry-rice and sat back with his beer. He was wearing what were for him unusually sporty clothes: light brown cotton slacks and an open-necked, short-sleeved shirt, but still looked drawn and tired.

The two men were in one of Noguchi's favourite haunts, in a back street not far from the harbour. Otani had been there often enough with him over the years for the fat woman proprietor to have paid no special attention to their presence beyond showing her fine collection of gold teeth in a cheery grin and ladling out bigger than usual helpings of curry for them. It was well after one o'clock and the little restaurant was emptying fast after the lunchtime rush, at its worst between noon and half past twelve.

''Not out of the wood yet. The old girl's statement will have to be corroborated. Not an unprejudiced witness, like I said. She's also quite a character, according to Hara.''

''Senile, you mean? Wandering in her mind?''

''He says not. Very spry for seventy, likes to get out and about. Scared of her daughter-in-law, though. Claims she wanted to make a statement when the original house-to-house enquiries were going on but Mrs O made her stay upstairs and threatened to wallop her if she made a sound. It's that upstairs room that overlooks a corner of the Hinomaru Building.''

''So she must have told Okada's wife before then what she saw.''

''Bound to have done. Urabe reckons Okada's missis is pretty sharp. Might even have seen something herself. He's going to work on her a bit more. Meantime Kimura's sniffing round a guy he saw at Dejima Pharmaceuticals.''

''Yes. He told me about him.''

Noguchi raised his almost non-existent eyebrows. ''Well,

111

well. I'd never have guessed. Anyway, that TV programme of yours has convinced him this whole bag of tricks is going to boil down to a drug deal."

Otani pulled a crumpled packet of Mild Seven cigarettes out of his shirt pocket and lit one. "It was just a passing thought. Let's go back a bit, though. I want to just check that I've got this straight, Ninja. First the background. Okada's mother knows full well her son's a *yakuza*, been working for Motoyama for years. Also probably knows that his 'confession' was a typical put-up job, to keep Motoyama himself out of jail. So she has a grudge against Motoyama. All that makes her statement very dodgy indeed."

"I already said that."

"Yes, I know. Bear with me, Ninja, I've got to try to keep my ideas straight. On the other hand, if there's anything at all in what she claims, at least you have some idea what it is you have to get corroborated. A lead, in other words. She genuinely picked out the photo? Wasn't . . . encouraged in any way?"

Noguchi looked almost shocked. "You know Hara. Belt and braces. He took along a big selection. Foreign women from Kimura's files. Mixed bag of Japanese men. Including your daughter's husband, cropped out from the family snap in the Dutch girl's bag. If it had been Kimura you'd be right to be leery, but—"

"All right. I agree with you. Besides, you said she'd already described Marianna van Wijk pretty accurately. Height, hair colouring, etcetera. And she's quite sure about the dates? Four days before the fire?"

"No doubt about it. First time was her grand-daughter's birthday, see? Old girl was on her way home with a present for her. Video of some Yank pop singer."

"And the old lady claims that Marianna van Wijk actually stopped her and asked her the way to the Hinomaru Building," Otani said thoughtfully. "Right, I can quite see that if that was what really happened she would have been intrigued enough to watch the foreigner go inside and then hang about in the travel agency opposite pretending to look through the brochures. About twenty minutes, she thought?"

112

"That's what she told Hara."

"And then the foreign woman came out and waved a taxi down, and a man tailed her?"

"That's another dodgy bit, of course. Always a *chinpira* or two hanging about outside any *yakuza* headquarters, specially these days. Could have been Gran's imagination about the tailing."

"Yes, and *chinpira* are just low-grade errand-boys and touts, after all. Not very bright as a rule. Motoyama would hardly use somebody like that if he wanted her followed. Did she describe the man? I'm sorry, Ninja, I realise all this is at one remove. I must say I wish you'd spoken to the old lady yourself."

"It might come to that. You could have a word with Hara, I suppose."

Otani shook his head regretfully. "I'm sorely tempted, but I don't want to put Hara on the spot. I think he'd have a problem with his official conscience if he even knew you and I were in contact like this. In a way I can't help respecting him for it, Ninja."

Noguchi nodded his bullet head almost imperceptibly. "He's a good lad, even if he is a bit green. Perhaps you're right. I'll have another go at him myself."

"Thank you. Let me just re-cap about the day of the fire. Mrs Okada Senior was in the upstairs room looking out of the window. Rather too convenient, wouldn't you say?"

"No. Spends hours there every day watching the world go by when she isn't nattering to the neighbours or round at the local police box telling them her troubles. Urabe got the same story independently from the daughter-in-law."

Otani sucked air in through his teeth, still a little dubious. "All right, I suppose it's quite possible. My wife's never had a mother-in-law to contend with, thank goodness. Anyway, an hour or so before the fire started she saw Marianna van Wijk again, turning the corner in the direction of the Hinomaru Building."

"Right."

"Just the woman. She's sure there was nobody else?"

"So it seems."

"I see. Shortly before the fire broke out, she saw a Japanese man running, definitely *running* away from that direction."

"That's what I was told."

"And she's certain that man was *not* Akira Shimizu?"

"Absolutely certain. They did make her look very carefully at his picture in particular. Nothing like him, Gran said. And went on to give a useful description. Got eyes in the back of her head, that old girl."

Otani bowed his head briefly. "May the gods be thanked," he said.

Chapter 15

"IT'S VERY KIND OF YOU TO SPARE THE TIME, MISS SHIRO-moto," Hanae said, fiddling with the clasp of her handbag. "I did try to explain on the telephone. It's very difficult for my daughter at the moment, you see. With her little boy at kindergarten. Otherwise she would have come to see you herself." Miserably aware that she always blushed when fibbing, she forced herself to look up into the tall young woman's eyes.

Miss Shiromoto laid a hand impulsively on Hanae's arm and squeezed it gently. "I'll be very pleased to help if I can," she said. "We're all naturally very concerned about Mr Shimizu."

"My . . . daughter was most insistent that I should offer you lunch," Hanae faltered, gesturing vaguely round the air-conditioned splendour of the lobby of the Osaka Royal Hotel.

"It's very kind of you to offer, but I have to be getting back in just a few minutes, I'm afraid."

Hanae closed her eyes momentarily in relief. She had dreaded the assignment from the moment Otani had ex-plained to her exactly what he wanted her to do, and doubted if she could have possibly carried it off while coping with the

115

solemn sophistication of the waiters in one of the Royal's several elegant restaurants.

"A . . . a cup of tea, then?"

"That would be nice. Thank you." The lobby waitress was pertly pretty but not in the least formidable, and the business of ordering two cups of tea gave Hanae the opportunity to pull herself together. Even though Miss Shiromoto had a warm, friendly telephone manner, Hanae had expected her son-in-law's secretary in person to be a glamorous, enamelled "office lady" of the kind featured in television commercials and soap operas. She was pleasantly surprised.

The young woman who had approached her at the agreed meeting place near the bookstall and introduced herself was tall and had nice legs but gave an impression of gawkiness rather than elegance. Her hair was something of a mess and her only make-up was a touch of lipstick, but her intelligent eyes illuminated an otherwise unremarkable face, and the directness of her smile and the straightforward, unembarrassed way she spoke was distinctly reassuring.

"I've never met Mrs Shimizu, of course. Just spoken to her on the phone once or twice. Poor thing, she must be worried to death." Miss Shiromoto sighed as she pressed the slice of lemon in her tea firmly against the side of the cup with her spoon. "But quite honestly, Mrs Otani, I really don't see how I can help. The president of the company himself called me to his office to ask if I had any idea where Mr Shimizu might have gone, but I honestly hadn't a clue."

Hanae gulped and took a deep breath. "You haven't been working for my son-in-law for very long, after all . . ."

"No. It's not four months yet. I was very proud to be chosen. Of course I'd never met him until then because I joined the company while he was in charge of the London office, but everybody who knew him before that told me how lucky I was."

On the way to meet Miss Shiromoto Hanae had screwed up enough courage to stick firmly to her brief, and nothing had been further from her mind than to depart from it in any way. Nevertheless, something suspiciously like a flicker of

116

disillusionment in the girl's expression as she spoke stimulated a spontaneous response.

"I agree with them," she said. "I know how lucky I am to have him as a son-in-law, you see. But my daughter did say that he's finding it hard to settle down now that they're back in Japan. So I don't suppose you've seen him at his best yet."

"It can't be easy after London." Miss Shiromoto smiled, tactfully it seemed to Hanae, who sighed.

"So nothing particular has happened that you know of in the past few weeks to upset him?"

"Nothing in the office so far as I know, Mrs Otani. But I'm only his secretary."

Hanae found it possible to smile quite naturally. "My husband always says that secretaries are the only people who really know what goes on in any office. But please forgive me, I don't want you to think I'm just a nosy old mother-in-law. It was a particular favour I came to ask you on my daughter's behalf."

"Of course. Anything I can do."

Hanae sensed that she was losing Miss Shiromoto's sympathy and began to flounder, blushing again furiously but bravely battling on. "It's just . . . just that there are a few old friends of his she wants to get in touch with. One of them . . . it's just possible, you see, that . . . but she has no idea where they are now. We—she wonders if by any chance Akira keeps a file of name-cards at the office . . ." Her voice cracked and she fumbled in her handbag for a paper handkerchief. At once the hand was squeezing her forearm again and the warmth returned to Miss Shiromoto's manner.

"Don't distress yourself, Mrs Otani. I'll do my best to help. As a matter of fact I take care of Mr Shimizu's file of *meishi* myself. He has hundreds and I know some of them go back many years, so you never know. They're all indexed, so it won't take me long to look through them. If you could just let me have the names I'll do it as soon as I get back. Then I could perhaps ring Mrs Shimizu at home if I can find any of them. Unless, a better idea, if you'd care to come with me and wait for a few minutes in the lobby of our building I could give you photocopies of any I might be able to turn up. I'm only sorry I can''t invite you up to the office . . .''

"I may say I've just had a thorough scolding from my wife, Kimura, and I expect I deserved it. All the same it was well worth it.''

"Don't keep me in suspense, Chief. After all, I did make it clear that I'd have been only too pleased to talk to his secretary myself.'' Kimura cradled the receiver to his ear more comfortably and reached for a note-pad.

"I don't doubt it. And my wife made it even clearer that she would have very much preferred not to. Nevertheless, she got at least part of what we wanted without raising the young woman's suspicions, and that's the great thing at this stage. Plus an unexpected bonus. Are you still there, Kimura?''

"Yes.''

"All right, I'm sorry. I'll come to the point. As we agreed, I gave my wife a list of about a dozen names to hand over. Some of them I could supply myself; people I know to be long-standing business acquaintances of his in other companies, for example. About his own age. Plus three names I have good reason to remember from the old days. Former political associates of my son-in-law who gave me almost as much trouble as he did. A couple of names my wife remembered them mentioning in connection with the choir they used to belong to. And my friend Motoyama and your friend Dr Murata.''

"No friend of mine, Chief, but I am taking more than a casual interest in him since I figured out that hint of yours about the TV programme. Do you mean to say Mrs Otani struck gold?''

"Not gold exactly, but she did bring back photocopies of name-cards the secretary turned up in his collection matching seven of the names on my list. You know, when I was in England I remember telling a detective sergeant in Cambridge about our Japanese custom of using name-cards and keeping other people's, and how useful we often find it in police work—''

"Chief. Are you deliberately trying to drive me out of my mind?"

"No. Very well. Not surprisingly, my son-in-law has *meishi* in his possession for most of the perfectly innocent people on the list. Also for one of his former radical friends, now a car salesman with Mazda. Now the interesting bit. I'm sitting here looking at photocopies of both Motoyama's and Murata's name-cards. Good job you picked up that publicity brochure at Dejima Pharmaceuticals with Murata's full name in it. Very uncommon Chinese characters used for the given name in both cases . . . must be the same person. But here's the important thing, Kimura. Murata's card describes him as a research student at Kobe University. In view of his present seniority, that must have been a good many years ago. Very likely the late sixties. I think you ought to put out a feeler to the Public Security Investigation Agency: see if they know anything about him."

Kimura stared in annoyance at his pencil, whose carefully sharpened point he had snapped in his surprise. Then he cleared his throat and spoke with some care into the telephone. "Funny you should say that, Chief. I was planning to contact the PSIA anyway. Well, I'm sorry I wasn't more enthusiastic about your idea earlier. That discovery alone certainly justifies it. I'll chase it up right away. But if you'll forgive my saying this, I can't see why you sound rather pleased about the idea that Shimizu's acquainted with Motoyama."

"I'm certainly not *pleased*, Kimura-kun, far from it. I have no idea what my son-in-law's involvement in all this business amounts to, but it would be naive to imagine that his disappearance is purely coincidental. I'd very much like to talk to Motoyama again myself in the light of this new development, but I realise that really would be asking for trouble from the prosecutor's office. In any case, it's time for him to be leant on hard, and Ninja's the man to do that. Perhaps you'd get him to give me a ring at home, would you?"

"Yes, of course. But I still—no, wait a minute. What about this bonus you mentioned?"

"You're right. That's what I'm really pleased about. The secretary came up with an extra name; one that wasn't on my list. Apparently a man called Aoki rang her up more than once the day before my son-in-law vanished, wanting to get hold of him. She told my wife he sounded a bit of a thug."

"You want us to find out if Motoyama's got an Aoki on his payroll?"

"Not necessary. At least, I don't think so. You see, while this bright girl—Shiromoto her name is—was going through the *meishi* file hunting up the names, she remembered the phone calls and out of curiosity looked to see if there was an Aoki among them. Well, she found two, and photocopied them along with the others. One's out of the reckoning completely, because I've met him myself now and then at Rotary. He's a senior manager in the Mitsubishi Bank and nobody could sound less like a thug. The other one's a long shot, but I have a pricking in my thumbs about him."

"Another former radical, you mean? I could check when I get hold of a friend of mine at the PSIA."

"Yes, and definitely no. I mean the name does ring a bell in that connection, but I definitely *don't* want you to mention it to the PSIA. And not even to Hara or Ninja for the time being. Keep it strictly to yourself, Kimura. I'm going to try out an idea I have on my daughter. If she thinks there might be anything in it, I'll go and have a quiet look for myself. But I don't want any help at this stage. It would probably be counter-productive, especially if I'm right. That's why I'm sorry to disappoint you, but I'm keeping Aoki's present occupation and whereabouts to myself. I know you could probably find out easily enough from the secretary, so all I can do is ask you not to. I'd like you to concentrate on Murata and leave me to worry about Aoki."

Chapter 16

NINJA NOGUCHI OWED HIS NICKNAME AND THE ALMOST superstitious awe in which he was held by most of Kobe's yakuza in large measure to his rare talent for making himself effectively invisible. His natural habitat was the shabbier back streets, the fringes of horse and bicycle race meetings, cheap stand-up bars and eating-houses. Following a natural inclination to do without a shave and wearing his ordinary scruffy and ill-assorted clothes was therefore usually all that was required for him to melt into the background. Those hoodlums and layabouts who knew him by sight tended to make themselves scarce if they did spot him, while even the more observant of the others never suspected for a second that the old bruiser was a senior inspector of police who knew much more about the organisation and current trends in their profession than they did.

When he had occasion to stray into more salubrious parts of town it was often enough for Noguchi to put on his venerable pair of workman's breeches with a purple woollen belly-band peeping above them, and tough rubberised boots with a separate compartment for the big toe. Thus attired and carrying a tool-box he could wander anywhere entirely unnoticed by passers-by: or by unscrewing the cover of an electrical junction-box and fiddling vaguely with its interior remain unobtrusively in place for hours if necessary.

Having to visit the district prosecutor that afternoon had called for extreme measures, though, and even his close colleagues at headquarters and the handful of others he called friends would have had difficulty in recognising the stately elderly gentleman proceeding through the enclosed Motomachi shopping street in the early evening. Not so very many years before, Motomachi had been to Sannomiya in Kobe what Bond Street is to Oxford Street in London, and here and there traces of its former style and elitist elegance remained. The development of the ultra-glamorous Sanchika Town complex underground at Sannomiya had shifted the smart centre of gravity decisively half a mile to the east, though, and although the traders of Motomachi were fighting back it was a losing battle: even the mighty Mitsukoshi Department Store faced with ever-declining sales figures had closed its branch there a few years earlier.

Noguchi's carefully pressed navy-blue serge suit certainly pre-dated the Sanchika Town development by a good many years and might well have come from one of the stodgier gentlemen's outfitters of Motomachi in its great days. Even after several hours of wear on a hot and sticky day his white shirt looked clean and comparatively unrumpled, the old-fashioned stiff collar and gloomily nondescript tie contributing to an effect of unassailable respectability. He looked like a prosperous shopkeeper or minor professional man: the proprietor of a long-established sake shop perhaps, or conceivably a funeral director. Noguchi's barrel-chest merged imperceptibly with his aldermanic belly without the intervention of a waist, but for a man of his bulk he had unexpectedly dainty feet, on which twinkled highly-polished black shoes which he had paid three hundred and fifty yen to have shined by an old woman, one of several with pitches outside the national railway station. Noguchi had known her for years and been pleased when she treated him as a perfect stranger and took his money afterwards with only a faint hint of puzzlement in her lined, walnut face.

He was in a quietly satisfied mood anyway, having got on

much better with the ambitious Mr Akamatsu than he had expected to. He realised that a good deal of the credit was due to his protégé Hara, who had prepared the impeccably orthodox progress report at the bottom of which Noguchi had impressed his seal and which the prosecutor read in his presence with visibly increasing respect before asking a few predictable questions which gave Noguchi no trouble at all. There had been a difficult moment when Akamatsu mentioned Otani's name in such a way that Noguchi had almost but not quite been forced into the lie direct. He had no moral objection to telling lies and often in his dealings with his shady clientele did so for tactical reasons, but similar tactical considerations had led to his ordaining to Hara and Kimura that all statements made to the prosecutor—especially in writing—were to be technically true. Withholding information was quite another matter in Noguchi's view, and when Hara protested at such casuistry he merely glared in silent balefulness at the young man until he finally shrugged in uneasy acquiescence.

The meeting over, Noguchi concluded that Akamatsu was both shrewd and sensible, mainly on the basis of the questions that he had not asked, and had said as much to Kimura when talking to him from a public telephone booth within minutes of emerging from the district prosecutor's office. "Giving us enough rope to hang ourselves with, I'd say," had been his verdict, before letting Kimura babble excitedly about the conversation he had been having with Otani during Noguchi's absence from headquarters.

Before talking to Kimura, Noguchi had been intending to return to his one-room flat above a cheap restaurant specialising in Korean "stamina" cuisine, bits of grilled liver, kidney and other delicacies shunned by the fastidious but widely reputed to do wonders for a man's potency. The news about Motoyama's name-card made him decide to remain in his unaccustomed finery, though.

Besides, it had been years since he had last disguised himself as a solid bourgeois citizen and the reaction of the shoe-shine lady at the station had tickled him. It would be interesting to see if he had a comparable effect on the gangster boss. Noguchi had therefore put a few more ten-yen coins in the phone box and made a call to the Elite Pachinko Hall; and Motoyama was expecting him at his makeshift temporary headquarters there in half an hour. He was early, as he had planned to be.

The pinball arcade was in a side alley no more than two hundred metres from the western end of Motomachi. Noguchi knew very well where it was, but anyone who didn't could in any case have headed unerringly in the right direction after emerging from the covered shopping street, guided by the characteristic racket generated by hundreds of steel balls cascading simultaneously down the glass-enclosed obstacle courses of dozens of garishly painted machines. Keen as the Japanese are on onomatopoeia, it was an imaginative soul who gave these inane devices the name *pachinko*. In fact the sound they produce is more like that of a mighty waterfall heard from a distance, and none too great a distance at that.

Although it was still full daylight the two-storey building was brilliantly illuminated both inside and out, its upper facade a kaleidoscopic neon extravaganza. The front of the ground floor was mostly of glass, so that the interior was in clear view from the street. Noguchi walked straight past, neither quickening nor slackening his sedate pace, and was gratified to notice that neither of the two men lounging in the open doorway gave him a second look, even though one of them certainly had good cause to remember him. Unusually for that part of town, the building occupied a small island site. To one side was a scruffy little Shinto shrine dedicated to the Inari deity of fruitfulness and prosperity, its vermilion paintwork cracked and discoloured, its zig-zag paper talismans hanging forlornly stained and torn and the stone image of its fox guardian lacking half a front leg. On the other side and to the rear of the Elite Pachinko Hall was a tiny parking lot offering space for no more than ten or a dozen cars at best, and which was currently dominated by a bloated black Cadillac of a certain age. Mr Motoyama had evidently arrived.

Noguchi retraced his steps and walked straight into the

124

pinball arcade. The two hoodlums stood aside politely to let him pass, and one of them even barked out a perfunctory word of welcome as Noguchi headed for the cash desk and paid for a plastic bowl of steel balls. There were about fifty machines like bagatelle boards set vertically in the place, arranged back-to-back in long rows and each with a plastic chair in front. In spite of the hour, nearly all were occupied, and it took Noguchi a few moments to find a place towards the back and settle himself.

He did not look particularly incongruous as compared with the other patrons of the place. In spite of the heat of the day there were several other men in suits and ties among those playing the machines as well as some in short-sleeved shirts and a few youths in T-shirts and jeans. There was also a fair number of women, nearly all of them middle-aged or elderly, and without exception respectably if rather shabbily dressed. Indeed the average age of the patrons was probably forty or more, and they had in common an appearance of trance-like absorption in what they were doing, which was to feed a more or less continuous stream of the shining steel balls into the aperture at the top of the machine and flip the handle which set each careering downwards, groping from time to time unseeingly for another handful from the plastic bowl positioned to receive the occasional bounty of fifty or a hundred more spewed out by the machine. Most were so practised that they achieved a rate of several a second: the thin-nosed, dead-eyed woman next to Noguchi was an adept whose hand movements were almost inhumanly fast and deftly coordinated.

Noguchi despised pachinko, but over the quarter century and more since it first captivated the blue-collar inhabitants of urban Japan had spent a good many hours pretending to play the machines, whose incessant noise made pachinko arcades quite good places for him to meet his contacts. A trick of acoustics made it possible for people at neighbouring machines to carry on a conversation audible to each other but to nobody else, and the proximty of the bowls of steel balls enabled a grubby note to be slipped in one direction or a small envelope containing a

125

few used five-thousand yen notes in the other with the utmost discretion. Noguchi therefore knew what to do, though his technique was methodical and deliberate rather than accomplished. Even so, over the next twenty minutes his machine disgorged several gratifying quantities of balls while he kept one eye on the entrance, and by the time he saw Motoyama emerge from an inner office near the cash desk and go over to the two minders at the door Noguchi had won several times his original stake.

He took his time about bearing his spoils over to the cashier and having them weighed, and then selecting his prizes: a packet of corn flakes and two toilet rolls. Instead of then selling them back for cash as most winners did he elected to take them with him, and the woman in charge packed them as tidily in a plastic carrier bag as any supermarket checkout assistant. The bag had on it a picture of a cute pink elephant and in bold red script the English words "Let's Go Jumbo!", and Noguchi dangled it unselfconsciously from his beefy fist as he went to the door where Motoyama looked angry and his henchmen were shaking their heads defensively.

"About time too," Noguchi growled, and the three whirled round and gaped at him. "I was getting fed up waiting."

Wordlessly Motoyama indicated the way to the office, but Noguchi surged remorselessly through the little group. "No. We'll go and sit in your Caddy round the back. Can't hear yourself think in here." He paused at the edge of the pavement outside and scowled at the two minders who had followed a reluctant Motoyama out. "Don't need their company, either. Send them off to get their eyes tested if I were you," he added to Motoyama. "Specially him. Tsuji. Tadashi Tsuji, isn't it? Probably wouldn't recognise his own mother these days."

Motoyama hesitated, all wary unease, and Noguchi withered him with a look. "Not *scared*, are you, boss? I'm all alone, sweetheart. What could be nicer than a little session with me in the back seat?"

"Give me the keys," Motoyama muttered to Tsuji, holding out his hand.

"That's better," Noguchi said approvingly, and without looking back set off in the direction of the car park, plastic bag swinging jauntily.

Chapter 17

"... **V**ERY WORRIED AND PREPARED TO DISCUSS A deal. So you see, it's beginning to come together at last," Hara said to Kimura, whose expressive face made it clear that he was none too pleased to learn that he had not himself been Noguchi's choice of confidant following his lengthy conference with the gangster Motoyama in the back of the Cadillac. "For your added information, I should have mentioned that Inspector Noguchi asked me to explain that he had intended to discuss all this with you but couldn't get hold of you by phone."

Kimura laughed loudly and almost sincerely, then pulled a face at Hara. "Oh no he didn't. You're a nice man, Hara, but a very bad liar. You don't have to spare my feelings where Ninja's concerned, I've known him much too long. As a matter of fact, I probably know more from getting it through you than if he had told me himself. I tell you honestly, I can't imagine what you two see in each other, but there's no accounting for tastes. Incidentally, do you mind if I mention something personal?" Hara looked tentatively shocked, like a virtuous lady not quite sure whether or not she has just heard an improper remark, but made no reply and Kimura pressed on. "It's not that I

128

mind in the least, but I think you ought to know it really bugs the Chief. The way you keep on saying 'for your added information', I mean.''

"Ah. I'm not surprised. It upsets my wife, too," Hara said with unexpected equanimity. "Especially since my daughter's caught the habit from me. I have to put a hundred yen in the Salvation Army collection box we keep at home every time I say it.''

"Oh." There seemed nothing else to say on that subject, so Kimura cleared his throat noisily and returned to the matter in hand. "All right. Just as long as you know. Now let me just make sure I've got this straight. Ninja is now satisfied that Motoyama arranged for the Hinomaru Building to be burned down for the sake of the insurance money—which of course he certainly won't get. But quite apart from the subsequent complications it was a very unsubtle job in any case. Motoyama's not ready to come clean yet, but Ninja thinks there was a reason for the sloppiness, right? That Motoyama knew full well that in the case of a piece of yakuza property both we and the insurance company would immediately suspect arson: that he therefore wanted to divert that suspicion to a rival mob in the hope of killing two birds with one stone, namely doing himself a bit of good in the current power struggle and also collecting a lot of money. But he didn't bargain on a death, and the death of a foreigner at that. Right so far?''

"Precisely. Motoyama insisted that the death of Marianna van Wijk had nothing to do with him or his men, and that he can't account for her presence in the Hinomaru Building on the day of the fire. The inspector nevertheless feels that he might have been choosing his words with some care and that he possibly knows something about her which could be important to us. The failure of Motoyama's plan and the prospect of facing personally a charge of aggravated arson leading to a fatality has obviously led him to reconsider his priorities, and as I've already said the indications now are that in return for certain assurances he might have one or two interesting things to tell us on that and other subjects. It seems he was a very worried man even before the interview in his car. But I digress. At some point the inspector asked Motoyama an obvious question, namely—"

"Namely, why was he in such particular need of the cost of a substantial four-storey office building and its no doubt overvalued contents all of a sudden that he was prepared to take a very big risk and also put up with a lot of genuine dislocation of his operations? Go through that bit again, Hara, would you? And by the way, I don't know what you call Ninja when you're on your own with him, but all this business about 'the inspector' gets me confused."

"My apologies. Well, all he was able to infer from Motoyama's general attitude and one or two ambiguous remarks was that there is a very big project under offer and that he has been, how shall I put it, bidding for it in competition with one of his rivals. That whoever secures the contract, as it were, will be able to dominate all the other contenders for control of the entire yakuza syndicate in western Japan. Unfortunately for Motoyama, though, the down payment seems to be beyond his means. A sum of the order of a quarter of a million American dollars was mentioned. Cash."

"Which would cost perhaps half as much again to have discreetly laundered from yen. The big league. And friend Motoyama's normal cash flow must be piggy-bank stuff by comparison. I see. But no clue about the nature of the project? Seed money of a quarter of a million bucks suggests either a colossal heist of some kind that would call for expensive hardware and manpower, or a persuasive bribe to somebody very well placed indeed. But why American dollars, I wonder?"

"I've been puzzling over that, too. We know that Japanese yakuza are operating in Hawaii and on the west coast of the United States, but . . ."

"But how could an American connection help Motoyama domestically?"

"I don't know. And nor does Insp—I mean Ninja."

Kimura shrugged and smiled a little ruefully at Hara. "If

I were a military man I'd consider opening a second front, Hara. See if anybody near the top of the other main gangs might come across with some information. The stakes seem to be high enough to justify our offering an attractive price for it.''

"Ah . . . Ninja has it in mind to do that. After he's discussed the situation with the superintendent.''

"Ah indeed. And how do you feel about that, my scrupulous friend?''

Hara shifted in his chair uncomfortably and a touch of colour came into his pale round face, but he held Kimura's sardonic gaze manfully. "I'm . . . I'm persuaded. That we need his advice. In spite of the problem of his son-in-law.''

"Good,'' Kimura said briskly. "I'm very pleased to hear it. It was getting altogether too complicated trying to remember what you were and weren't supposed to know. Right. Since we've touched on the subject of Shimizu, tell me what Ninja got out of Motoyama in that connection. Do we have any idea yet how one of his name-cards came to be in Shimizu's collection?''

"So far, so good,'' Aoki said. "Now we come to Motoyama. How did a respectable businessman like you come to be in touch with a crook like him? Don't tell me you've reached the point of sharing his political principles?''

"I'm tired of you, Aoki. And very nearly at the end of my tether. If you want to know, listen and I'll tell you. But spare me your cheap wisecracks.'' Shimizu raised his head wearily and looked briefly into the other man's bloodshot eyes. He had not had access to a mirror since being under Aoki's control, but imagined that his own must look much the same. It was some small comfort to know that Aoki too was under strain.

"Go on, then. I'll listen.''

"Marianna and I met him at the same time. I've already explained that when her attachment to Dejima Pharmaceuticals began Marianna went to stay with her friend Penny Johnston.''

"The English girl."

"Yes. And you also know that Penny was already giving English conversation classes at the company. Twice a week, I think. And having an affair with Murata, the research director there. Not being a scientist, Marianna spent most of her time studying the financial, marketing and personnel management sides of the business, but had obviously been shown over the research and production facilities and met Murata right at the outset. Marianna made it clear to me that she'd told Penny in confidence about our relationship, and Penny made no secret of the fact that she was sleeping with Murata. She couldn't very well, since Murata was spending several nights a week at the flat."

"What did Murata's wife say to that?"

"He isn't married."

Shimizu's head drooped and he closed his eyes briefly, but the rasping voice of the interrogator gave him no respite. "Well, get on with it! We haven't got all night."

"I was . . . with Marianna at the flat early one evening, soon after she'd moved in. And Penny came back bringing Murata with her. So I was introduced to him. It was a shock. Because it was *our* Murata. From the old days."

In other circumstances Shimizu might have enjoyed the effect his revelation had on Aoki. As it was he tried not to cringe, half-expecting a stinging slap in the face. In the event Aoki remained silent for several seconds and then continued speaking in a calm, controlled way.

"Well, well, you *have* been saving up the best bit, haven't you? The Molotov cocktail man himself. Embarrassing for you."

"It could have been, I suppose, if they'd walked in half an hour earlier. He recognised me right away and wanted to know what I was doing these days, but was too full of himself to take in anything I said. Both he and the English girl seemed to be in a very excited frame of mind anyway, said they were going out to celebrate something or other and that they'd come to insist that Marianna and I should join them."

132

"What was your impression of Murata nearly twenty years on?"

"I disliked him as much as I ever had. Still very hail-fellow-well-met, arrogant, pleased with himself."

"A man very like yourself by the sound of it, comrade. As you were before I decided you had to be disciplined, anyway. And what were the happy couple celebrating?"

"They wouldn't say. Marianna had told me that Penny at least was in love and hoping to marry him. I suppose I imagined they'd decided to get engaged. Anyway, it would have been churlish to refuse the invitation, so we went with them to an expensive Chinese restaurant in Osaka. Somewhere in Dotombori. During the meal Murata got pretty drunk and started talking vaguely about a scientific breakthrough. Then this man Motoyama turned up and sat down as though he owned the place—"

"He probably does," Aoki said quietly.

"Very likely. But I didn't know that at the time. Murata was obviously expecting Motoyama. Introduced him as the man he was going to make a fortune for and who was going to make his in return."

"And Motoyama?"

"Oily, expansive but clearly uneasy. I got a strong impression that Marianna and I were far from welcome. All the same, he gave the two women and me one of his name-cards each. President, Hinomaru Enterprises, it said. Murata kept winking at him and asking how the fund-raising was going. Was he going to be invited to the bar-becue? One inane remark after another. Penny seemed to find him uproariously funny as Murata obviously did himself. Motoyama looked furious and tried to shut him up, then called for cognac by the tumblerful and fairly obviously tried to get us all so drunk we wouldn't remember a thing. Would to God he'd succeeded. If he had Marianna might still be alive today."

"But he didn't."

"No. Murata and Penny were pretty well incapable by the time we left. I tried to pay the bill but Motoyama waved me away. He'd also laid on a big hire car and we all went back

133

to Penny's flat. Marianna and I got the other two inside and let them more or less pass out on Penny's bed. I didn't want to leave her with them but Marianna insisted she could cope and that I should go home. So I did."

"And in the next few days you made a few enquiries about Motoyama, right?"

"Yes. I'd decided already that Motoyama was at the very least a very shady character and wondered what he and Murata could be up to, but left to myself I would have kept well clear of both of them. Marianna was actively worried, though. She hadn't liked the look of Motoyama any more than I had, and put two and two together much more quickly. She asked me to find out what I could about Motoyama, and within the constraints of her study programme at Dejima Pharmaceuticals did what she could to keep an eye on Murata. It wasn't too difficult for me to confirm my suspicion that Motoyama might be a yakuza boss."

"How did you do that? I'm curious." Aoki's manner was now patient, almost friendly.

"The next time I was having a few drinks with some contacts of mine from the Chamber of Commerce I brought the conversation round to the subject of the legislation against *sokaiya*. Everyone agrees it doesn't work. A gangster still has to buy only a handful of shares in his own name and those of a few of his hoodlums to have the right to attend the AGM of a public company, and the facts of life are unchanged. Whatever the law says, if he isn't paid off he and his friends will wreck the proceedings, but if he is, the gang makes sure everything goes smoothly."

"By intimidating and silencing individual shareholders with genuine questions or grievances. And that's the 'democratic capitalism' you've sold out to, Shimizu. Can you wonder why we despise you?"

"I've never said capitalism's democratic. I'm trying to tell you how I checked Motoyama out. I know my own company pays *sokaiya* protection money to an Osaka-based gang, and volunteered the name. My friends were taken aback at first. These things aren't generally talked about openly. Then one by one they came across. And one of the gangs mentioned was called Hinomaru, run by a man called Motoyama.''

"Quite the detective, aren't you?'' The sneering note was back. "And your fellow sleuth did equally well with Murata?''

"Yes, she did. Marianna was on good terms with the head of personnel at Dejima Pharmaceuticals and he let one or two things slip which convinced her that something about Murata was bothering him. But not surprisingly she got much more out of her friend Penny . . .''

"So to cut a long story short, Ninja wants the two of us to sort out the Dejima Pharmaceuticals side of things.''

"That is so, yes. He would be grateful if you would see Miss Penny Johnston again and ask her what she knows about Akira Shimizu's present relationship with Dr Murata. We know of course that they were political associates in the sixties, but thanks to you we now also know that the Public Security Investigation Agency has no current interest in either of them. It is of course conceivable that Miss Johnston herself was innocently instrumental in putting them in touch with each other again after so many years.''

"Yes. It had occurred to me. I'll bear it in mind.''

"I meant no offence. Everybody respects your skills in handling foreign witnesses, Inspector. Especially—''

"Especially young women. So you all should.'' Kimura grinned, by no means displeased. "And what are you going to be up to while I work my magic on Penny-san, may I ask?''

"Ninja thinks that I should become acquainted with Dr Murata as soon as possible.''

"Interview him, you mean?''

"Not formally. In an ingenious way suggested by the superintendent after talking to an influential—and perhaps rather unexpected—friend of his. I'm sure you would agree that Dr Murata may well be of much more use to us at this stage if he remains off guard. You have already described him as an arrogant man. Such people tend to un-

135

derrate the intelligence of others, and we feel that it should not be beyond ours to discover what this gifted pharmacological researcher's game is. You catch my drift, I hope.''

Kimura looked at the younger man with new respect. ''Yes. I fancy I do. I'll bear it in mind when I talk to Penny Johnston.''

Chapter 18

IN THE TINY GARDEN OF THE OLD HOUSE AT THE FOOTHILLS of Mount Rokko Otani pretended to brood over one of his bonsai. It was a miniature pine of no great age but already satisfactorily gnarled, and might in a few years be fit for display at the annual show of the Rokko Bonsai Club of which Otani was a proud former President; but he scarcely saw it, for in fact he was keeping an eye on the kitchen.

Through the open door he could hear Hanae assuring their daughter that she and young Kazuo could perfectly well manage the local shopping between them, and Kazuo chiming in eagerly to confirm that he would carry his Obaa-chan's bag for her. Some time had elapsed since Hanae had popped her head out to tell her husband they were off but it was never easy for her to make a decisive departure from anywhere, and Akiko had inherited her taste for last-minute conversations. After a while Otani therefore turned his attention to his beloved juniper and snipped at it delicately here and there until at last he heard the front door rattle open and closed, and the voices of Hanae and their grandson in animated conversation as they made their way down the road. Even then Akiko took her time about joining him in the garden.

Otani put down the tiny, razor-sharp secateurs which had

belonged to his father, stretched and tightened the old silk sash round his faded blue and white yukata and looked at his daughter. Akiko seemed smaller than usual. He realised that it was because he was wearing wooden *geta*, their platforms raised on inch-high blocks, while she had slipped her bare feet into the pair of flat plastic sandals Hanae kept at the back entrance. All the same, the unfamiliar disparity in their height intensified the feeling of protective love which swept through him. Akiko was pale and looked tired, but managed a small smile. "Try not to look so sorry for me, Father," she said. "It makes it harder."

"Come and sit down. I need your help." Otani sat on the sun-warmed wooden step formed when the glazed sliding outer panels of the back room were open as they were that day. Akiko hesitated and then sat beside him in the sunshine. From the upper rooms of the house it was possible on a clear day to see the Inland Sea, but they had a view only of a vista of blue- and red-tiled roofs and a petrified forest of television aerials. "You see, I think I may know where he is." He heard Akiko's sharp intake of breath, but for several seconds she said nothing. When she did speak her voice was unsteady, but seemingly under reasonable control.

"He's all right, then?"

"I can't say for sure yet, but I'm reasonably confident. I'm hoping to find out today, if you're willing to answer a few quite simple questions." Otani sought her eyes with his, wondering if even admitted strain and unhappiness could break down a barrier which he had failed to pass or undermine over many years.

"Of course. If I can. What do you want to know?"

"It means going back a long way. To your student days, when you first knew Akira. Funny, isn't it? He's never minded talking to me about those times, but you've always refused." Akiko had already turned her head away and Otani thought he could feel the tension in her.

"Because it's all in the past, Father. It should stay there."

"I'm afraid that isn't the way things work, Aki-chan."

"Akira isn't in some kind of political trouble, is he?"

"Not so far as I know. In some danger, perhaps."

138

Akiko stood up and stared out over the rooftops, her back to her father, then abruptly wheeled round to face him. "Very well. What do you want to know?"

"Basically, as much as possible about some of Akira's former political associates. Principally a man called Aoki."

"Makoto Aoki?"

"You obviously remember him. Yes, Makoto Aoki."

"What about him?"

"Whatever you can tell me. For a start, what did he look like?"

A faraway look had come into Akiko's face, and Otani was disconcerted to feel the pricking of tears at the back of his own eyes as he saw the ghost of the ardent girl she had been in the features of the mature, until recently confident woman who was his daughter. She remained silent for some time and then spoke calmly at first, caressing the needles of the little pine tree with the back of her hand. Otani doubted if she was aware of doing so.

"He was . . . amazingly ugly. His head was too big for his body. His face was covered with horrible spots. He had a harsh, noisy way of talking. We used to say that his voice had no volume control . . ." Then her voice trailed off uncertainly and the next sound Otani heard was a sniff as she fumbled in the pocket of her cotton dress and took out a paper handkerchief. At once he got up and put his arm round her shoulders: the first time he had touched her for a very long while.

"I'm sorry, my dear. I'm not deliberately keeping you in suspense, you know. It's just that . . . I must be sure before I raise your hopes too much."

Akiko's head came up proudly, she pulled away and stopped dabbing at her eyes. "You're not very subtle, Father. I presume from what you've been saying that Akira's probably with Aoki again. If so, I don't quite understand what you mean by 'hopes'. I'm certainly not going chasing after him. It's for Akira to get in touch with me if and when he chooses."

"Yes. I understand what you mean, of course. It's still not much more than a guess anyway, but it interests me that you

139

don't sound particularly surprised. How close was Aoki to Akira in the old days?''

Akiko laughed, but there was neither warmth nor humour in it. ''At first, very. Akira used to call him his conscience. It made Aoki furious. It was always easy to wind him up by teasing him about his first name. 'Mr Sincerity Greentree' we used to call him in English, then wait for the inevitable lecture about 'integrity'.''

The sounds were meaningless to Otani. ''Is that how you translate Makoto Aoki? I suppose it's a joke of some kind. Still, it's hard for a boy to live up to a first name like that. What was his role in Akira's faction?''

''It's hard to say.''

''You say Akira called him his conscience. Does that mean he was the ideologist of the group?''

Akiko laughed again, and it sounded a little less forced than before. ''Oh, no. We were all specialists in ideology. Aoki was . . . well, a kind of *coach* almost, if that makes any sense. He always seemed to be the first to notice when anybody began to flag, or lose interest. His talent was to keep people up to the mark, and he was good at it because he varied his technique to suit whoever he was dealing with.''

''I'm sure I never met him,'' Otani said thoughtfully. ''I would have remembered if I had. How long is it since you saw or heard from him, Aki-chan?''

''Me? It must be well over ten years. Not since Akira and I were married, certainly.''

''But Akira kept in touch with him? No, don't clam up now, I beg you.'' Otani watched her restless fingers working at the cotton skirt as the silence seemed to push them apart. Then Akiko's shoulders slumped.

''Yes, he did go on seeing him. Sporadically. Often a whole year or more would go by between meetings. In case you're wondering, Akira always told me. I'm sure of that.''

''So you know what became of Aoki, then? After university. Quite a startling development.''

Akiko shook her head slowly. ''Not really. Quite logical from the point of view of anyone who knew him. How did you get on to him?''

140

"Oh, there were one or two pointers . . ." Otani's manner was vague as he stood up and pottered back to the row of bonsai. "The question is whether Akira wants to be found, as it were. Assuming we're right about all this, of course. And I intend to find that out one way or the other before long."

"Father. 'In some danger', you said. What do you mean? You don't seriously think Akira had anything to do with that Dutchwoman's death, do you?"

Secateurs in hand, Otani wheeled round and stared at his daughter.

"If you mean do I think he killed her, no, certainly no. But I think he may know who did, and that the murderer is aware of the fact. That is what I meant by saying that I think he might be in some danger, rather than running away from you."

Akiko closed her eyes and lowered her head for a moment, then looked up again. "I suppose I ought to be relieved. And I am, of course. But whatever happens it's finished, isn't it? Between me and Akira, I mean."

Otani shook his head slowly. "If things turn out as I hope, that will be for you to say, Aki-chan. But I think you'd be wrong to decide anything. Certainly not at this stage when there are so many unanswered questions. One important fact at least is known: the lady in the case is dead. Whatever harm she may have done you is in the past. Think about it." He reached out a tentative hand as though to caress her head but pulled back without doing so. "I'm going inside to get dressed now, then I'll be off. Tell your mother I'm not sure when I'll be back, will you?"

"Are you going to talk to him, Father?"

"I don't know yet. The main thing is to find out if he really is there, and somehow I don't think anybody would tell me over the telephone. If I'm right I shall know what to do next. Apart from something else I've already put in hand, I mean."

Murata looked round quickly and satisfied himself that none of his staff was within earshot before he picked up the telephone. There were two instruments on his desk, and it was rare to receive a call on his direct outside line because he was careful about whom he divulged the number to. Both Penny Johnston and his other current mistress knew it—though not of each other's status—but he had made it clear to them that contact during working hours was unwelcome. He thought it likely that his caller was someone else: Motoyama probably, or one of two other men who had in recent weeks had a privileged claim on his attention. He was mistaken. The voice was unfamiliar, attractively husky and obviously that of a young woman.

"Good afternoon! Kansai Television here. May I speak to Dr Murata, please?"

"This is Murata speaking. Kansai Television, did you say?"

"That's right. Hello there, *sensei*! My name is Sayoko Irie, researcher for the *Fumio Iwai Looks Sideways At . . . Life* show. I have the right person, I hope? This is the distinguished scientist Dr Murata? The inventor of Gynojoy?"

"Well, 'inventor' is hardly the word. We researchers work as a team here, Miss, er . . ."

"Irie. But please call me Sayoko. We don't stand on ceremony in the media."

"I see. Well . . . Sayoko, I can't say I've watched the Fumio Iwai show very often, but I've heard of it, of course. Let me explain that the Gynojoy formula has been perfected as a result of intensive collaborative research here in the Dejima Pharmaceutical Company's laboratories, but yes, I suppose it would be true to say that I—"

"You're so *modest*! Well, *I'm* certainly grateful to you personally, Doctor. And so are a lot of other girls I know. Not to mention our boyfriends!"

Murata held the receiver a little away from his ear as the creamy laughter continued, and smoothed his moustache with his free hand. "That's very gratifying," he said after a suitable interval. "And what can I do for you?"

"Oh, my, if you really look like your picture in the company brochure I can think of lots of things! But right now, I'm calling to say that Fumio Iwai has been planning for some time now to *Look Sideways At . . . Mankind's Modest Bene-*

factors. A group of programmes each introducing as a special guest someone whose work has improved the quality of life here in Japan but who may not have received proper recognition. And one name on everybody's shortlist here at the studio is yours, Doctor!''

''Oh, really, Sayoko. I hardly think . . .''

''Oh, come now, you can't be surprised. Maybe Fumio himself didn't think of you right away, but we're nearly all women on the research team and I can tell you that Gynojoy is the tops as far as we're concerned. So please say yes. Say you'll be the first *Modest Benefactor*. Please?''

''Well, I . . . I should have to discuss it with the president of the company . . .''

''Whatever for? He'll be *thrilled*, *sensei*. Fumio Iwai isn't shy about mentioning brand names, you know. So quite apart from ensuring that you get the recognition you deserve it'll be a massive publicity boost for Dejima Pharmaceuticals. But the whole point is that it's *you* we want, the backroom genius who made the breakthrough, not your president muscling in to claim the credit. You don't mind my speaking frankly like that?''

''No, of course not.'' Murata's fingers caressed his moustache again. ''I'll certainly think about it, Sayoko. Um . . . strictly hypothetically, if I were to agree, what exactly would it entail?''

''A couple of hours of your time is all, Doctor. We'll videotape a run-through interview first—in your laboratory there if you like—then play it back to you so you can see how it goes. A kind of rehearsal a couple of days before the live show. You will do it, won't you? If a grateful Gynojoy user asks you *very* nicely? Over a drink this evening perhaps?''

Inspector Hara remained silent and motionless as Woman Senior Detective Junko Migishima worked on the scientist for a little longer, agreed a time and place for their rendezvous and finally rang off. Then he reached forward, switched the recorder attached to the telephone to fast re-wind and ran the tape back so that they could both listen to the conversation again. Junko frowned once or twice at some of her own

143

words but mostly listened with a twisted little smile on her lips, while Hara nodded judiciously from time to time.

"A bit over the top," she admitted when Hara switched off the machine. "But he's so vain I could have laid it on even thicker. Did you hear him at the end, sir? You could practically see his tongue hanging out."

"Undoubtedly a very satisfactory performance, officer. Well done. I'm a little surprised that he didn't ask you how you obtained his direct-line telephone number. You know what to say if he does so this evening."

"Sure. TV researchers have their methods. No doubt he believes that implicitly anyway. Nice of the real Sayoko Irie to let me use her name."

"Indeed. In the unlikely event of Murata's ringing Kansai Television and asking for her she will take a message from him, ostensibly on your behalf. So only she and Mr Iwai himself are parties to the deception, and Superintendent Otani assures me that the discretion of both is assured."

Junko looked at her superior with a new respect. "It's pretty risky, sir," she said happily. "The district prosecutor will hit the roof if he ever finds out."

Inspector Hara took off his granny glasses and polished them thoroughly before replying. "Perhaps. But then, you see, it is by no means certain that he will," he said. "I have not been acquainted with the superintendent for as long as you have, officer, but I am learning that his occasionally unorthodox methods have many advantages, and that it is wise to act upon his suggestions when possible. I have every confidence that at the end of your conversation with him this evening you will leave Dr Murata in a suitably unguarded frame of mind."

"I'll do my best, sir."

Junko sprang lightly to her feet and stood to attention as Hara disentangled his ungainly body from his chair.

"I'm sure you will. Well, er, carry on, Mrs Migishima. If you will forgive the ambiguity of the phrase."

"Sir!" Junko made no attempt to hide her grin as she moved to the door.

"One moment, Mrs Migishima, if you please."

She turned to face him again, startled to see a dull pink nush in his normally pallid cheeks. "Yes, sir?"

"I don't quite know how to put this, but . . . do you . . . that is, are you personally of the opinion that this product, Gynojoy, what I mean is—"

"Does it work?' Junko's eyebrows shot up and she pulled at one earlobe, at the same time twisting her wide, generous mouth into a comically quizzical smile. "Well, I wouldn't say it doesn't."

Hara nodded pensively. "Thank you. My wife suffers greatly, you see, and . . ."

"Tell her from me to give it a try," Junko said briskly. "Or else just keep out of her way as much as you can once a month."

He was still standing there nodding his head as she closed the door behind her.

Chapter 19

THE KINKI NIPPON RAILWAY COMPANY, BETTER KNOWN as the Kintetsu Line, is the biggest of the commercially operated railway networks established by speculators early in the century to supplement and to profit from the expanding national network administered by officials of the government. They prospered mightily by encouraging city folk to live at ever-increasing distances from their places of work, in suburbs developed very often by the railway companies themselves in order to take back in fares a goodly proportion of the money the new-style commuters saved on the cost of their accommodation.

The lively-minded entrepreneurs behind the Kintetsu Line did well enough from the first by ferrying people between the cities of Osaka and Nara, and even better when some years later they extended their operations as far as the ancient capital of Kyoto. Then they cast their eyes far eastwards towards the rich pickings to be had on the other side of the Kii peninsula. Their engineering consultants sucked their teeth at the thought of the horrendous problems involved in constructing a line through the mountainous terrain of Mie Prefecture, but land there was cheap in those days and the cost of labour hardly worth taking seriously. So by 1938 the thing was done, and from those days onwards little stopping trains have waited humbly at stations in out-of-the-way places to allow glossy "special expresses" to thunder through laden with pilgrims on their way to the hallowed Shinto shrines at Ise, vacationers bound for the seaside resort and cultured-pearl centre of Toba, and countless others with business in the great city of Nagoya itself. Renowned if less glamorous places of pilgrimage abound along the route, and many of the intermediate stations are called by the names of nearby temples and shrines.

It was at one such that Otani alighted in the mid-afternoon. The only other passengers to do so were a sharp-looking young man in casual clothes that looked brand-new, his girl-friend who was wearing a black vinyl skirt as tight as it was short with an incongruously frilly blouse, and a kimono-clad old lady with a sharp-cornered package wrapped in cloth, which she brandished like an offensive weapon as she bustled towards the exit muttering to herself and casting a deeply suspicious look at Otani as she passed him.

The village served by the station was tucked in a valley among the shaggy Yoshino mountains, but even so it was several hundred feet above sea-level and there was a fresh-ness in the air which raised Otani's spirits a little: a small enough encouragement to set against the depression he had been fighting for the past few days even as the pieces of the jig-saw had begun to fall into place.

He took a deep breath as he walked out of the station and looked about him. The old lady was already halfway into the lone taxi waiting in a forecourt scarcely big enough for it to turn round in. To one side there was a ramshackle open-fronted souvenir shop with a huge soft-drink-dispensing ma-chine outside. The young man and his girl made for it and chose Fanta orange and grapefruit drinks respectively, which made Otani conscious of his own thirst. He treated himself to a Dr Pepper, drank it down and deposited the can tidily in the nearby bin. Burping discreetly, he then went over to join the couple by a large display board near the bank of ticket machines at the station entrance. Its centrepiece was a pic-torial map of the vicinity with dotted lines indicating a number of recommended rambles and notes giving the length of each and the time needed to accomplish it: while to one side was a panel on which were painted advertisements for three local inns.

Otani waited patiently while the citified pair ahead of him peered dubiously at the map and discussed possibilities, and watched them set off after a while, the young man forging ahead while the girl teetered behind him on her high heels. Then he took their place at the display board and shook his head in gentle sorrow as he saw for himself the line of the hike they had loudly agreed upon. He doubted if either the girl's shoes or her ankles would survive more than a few hundred metres of stony mountain path, and they had set themselves a demanding circuit timed to take an hour and fifty minutes.

His own destination was clearly marked as an important stage on a shorter and less hilly route beginning on the other side of the station itself, and he estimated that it should take him no more than fifteen or twenty minutes to reach it. Indeed, when he had made his way over the level-crossing which bisected the road to the village below and now behind him he thought he could see the place, half-hidden in the middle distance on the flank of the thickly wooded mountainside ahead. There was even an unpainted wooden signpost with incised lettering to direct him to it beside a roadside image of the boddhisatva Jizo, where a narrow but well-made path veered off between tiny, terraced rice-fields towards the uncultivated slope two or three hundred metres beyond.

Otani paused before the little statue on its low plinth in a ramshackle open-fronted wooden structure. Less than a metre high, it had been amateurishly chiselled in stone of the kind he could see outcropping from the hillside above, but was of an antiquity which had endowed it with a certain dignity. A dirty jam-jar holding a few drooping flowers stood on the base in front, while round the neck of the image were several bibs, one on top of another, of the kind small children wear when eating their meals. These had all originally been red in colour, but the lower ones had faded to a pinkish grey

148

where exposed to the sunlight and even the uppermost was far from pristine. Otani decided that the children of the village must either be particularly robust and thus in no need of Jizo-sama's intercession to help them recover from illness or of his kindly protection in the Buddhist hell after their death: or much more likely that in these days of "negative population growth", as Hara called it, they were very few in number.

Otani indulged in a few superstitions and liked to see old customs kept up but was in no sense a religious man. All the same, as he stood there the eager face of his grandson rose up in his mind's eye. Almost unaware of what he was doing he bowed his head before the image, and something between a wish and a prayer for young Kazuo and for the mother who was his own only child momentarily linked him with the piety and the emotions of the country people who generations before had erected the statue where locals and wayfarers alike must pass it.

Then he braced himself and set off along the path. In the heat of the afternoon the little rice-fields painstakingly clawed from the foot of the mountain gave off a dank, secret smell but they were soon behind him, and once fairly among the trees Otani sniffed appreciatively at the resinous tang in the air. The path wound quite steeply upwards and he took his time, pausing several times to wipe the sweat off his forehead and listen to the small, mysterious sounds around him. He saw several gecko lizards dart away to safety as he approached the rocky outcrops on which they had been crouched, and once a snake: a little jewelled thong of beauty gliding serenely among the loose stones that often made his own footsteps uncertain and threatened a twisted ankle.

Now and then a turn in the path afforded a glimpse of the dull metallic grey of roof tiles between the trees, and before long Otani came to a long flight of stone steps rising up to his right. The path continued on past them, but another wooden signpost confirmed that he had arrived. As if acknowledging the fact, the dull boom of a Buddhist temple bell reverberated above him as he began to toil up the steps, and its tolling continued until he reached the formal gateway, its timbers aged to a silver-grey and its roof-thatch of rice-straw blotched with the cool velvety green of lichen.

It was a bigger place than he had expected, with tile-roofed plastered walls stretching away to either side of the entrance and what was obviously a considerable complex of buildings partially visible beyond the main hall facing Otani at the other side of a sizeable forecourt. Although the massive gates themselves were fastened back and looked as though they had not been closed for many years, a low portable barrier of bamboo was in place across the gap: easily circumvented but less than welcoming. The bell was now silent and Otani hesitated. For all its physical inadequacy the bamboo barrier was eloquently forbidding, and he found himself doubting the wisdom of what he was doing: wondering whether he was in fact justified in violating a sanctuary.

As he stood there indecisively a man emerged from the dark shadows of the main hall opposite, slipped his bare feet into a pair of straw sandals at the top of the wooden stairs leading down to ground level and set off across the forecourt, pausing when he caught sight of Otani standing indecisively outside the gate.

"*Yokoso,*" he said. "*Onobori-yasu.* You are welcome. Pray make the ascent."

It was years since Otani had heard the quaint phrase used to encourage mountain pilgrims, and he found it curiously soothing. He bowed, stepped round the barrier and bowed again after approaching the man. He was a priest, his shaven head bluish in the sunlight, a pouch-like square of undyed cloth with ivory rings at the upper corners suspended from his neck and worn at his chest over his plain black kimono.

"You must be hot and tired," the priest then said. "Come with me and drink some green tea."

Otani began to protest politely but the priest had already set off so he trailed after him round a corner of the main hall to another building, clearly living quarters of some kind. At the entrance the priest slipped his feet out of his sandals while Otani took off his own shoes, and offered him a pair of back-

150

less plastic slippers, which Otani declined. The room to which the priest took him was austerely dignified, the tatami matting cool to Otani's stockinged feet, the only incongruity the large wide-necked vacuum flask which was placed on a metal tray with a few upended handleless cups directly on the matting near the *tokonoma* alcove in which was displayed a calligraphic scroll of the kind Otani could never decipher. The tea was cold; not chilled so as to impair its fragrance, but refreshingly cool and astringent, and Otani gratefully accepted a second cup which like the first was drunk in a silence which felt companionable. Then the two men looked at each other, and both knew.

"I am most interested to meet you, Superintendent Otani," the priest said.

"And I you, Aoki-*sensei*. May I ask how you recognised me?"

"Your daughter Akiko-san is, if I may say so, more beautiful than you, but her eyes and her mouth are yours. Besides, I've been expecting you."

"He is here, then?"

"Yes. He's here. Come."

Aoki rose to his feet with a fluidity of motion that was almost graceful in such an ungainly, coarse-featured man and Otani followed him out of the room and along a polished wooden corridor. The sliding panels to one side were fully opened and they passed first a small side-garden: a minor masterpiece of artfully contrived wilderness in miniature, complete with precipices and waterfalls, craggy mountains a foot or two high, lush valleys of moss and mysterious groves of delicate bamboo.

Rounding the corner of the building, Otani saw the main walled garden at the back. It was much larger; some thirty by fifteen metres and designed in the classic Zen style with a number of boulders of irregular shape and differing considerably in size, embedded apparently at random in a sea of pale, almost white gravel. Patches of natural discoloration, and of green, brown and yellow lichen here and there on the boulders with a ragged fringe of moss at their base provided the only touches of colour, but the total effect was not only one of great beauty but also of life and motion. It was, Otani knew, simply enough achieved, by raking the gravel into a design of gentle ridges. Each free-standing boulder or group of two or three was an island surrounded by eddies reflecting the contours of its base while the greater expanse of gravel was raked into straight lines.

It was tricky work, and Otani was not surprised that the man in the tattered kimono working with his rake at one corner of the garden did not look up when he and Aoki began to converse quietly.

"You haven't made him shave his head, then."

"No. He's not a monk. Strictly speaking he should still be crouching in silence outside the gate waiting to be admitted. It was nearly seventy-two hours before the old master let me in years ago, and I fancy my frame of mind was a good deal more receptive than your son-in-law's was. For the first day or two at least."

"He seems tranquil enough now." Otani experienced something very like anger at the sight of his wife's husband lovingly teasing the gravel into place while a tormented Akiko cared for their son and fought to retain her dignity.

Aoki looked at him. "You're bitter, and very far from being at peace yourself, Superintendent," he said, and Otani glared back.

"Quite right. And I don't expect to be in the foreseeable future. So. Now that you've broken him you'll make him a monk, I suppose? And he'll stay here."

"I'm not sure, but I don't think so. He'd no doubt rather stay here than go to jail for murder, of course . . ."

"Don't be ridiculous. He's no murderer."

Aoki nodded, his face grave. "I'm very glad to hear you say that. I presume that is both a personal and an official opinion?"

"It is."

"That's very satisfactory. I think we should now talk this over properly, don't you? Your son-in-law can, I think, be persuaded at last to tell you a number of things you may not know." Aoki raised his voice. "Shimizu-kun!" The man in

152

the corner at once stopped work, turned in their direction and bowed, then stood humbly with eyes lowered.

"Come over here! We have matters to discuss with the father of your wife."

Chapter 20

"IT WAS VERY GOOD OF YOU TO AGREE TO SEE ME AT such short notice," Kimura said politely as Penny Johnston stood back to allow him into her apartment. He was looking forward to forming a clearer impression of her lifestyle on the fifth floor of a featureless block he judged had been built perhaps twenty years earlier; and on arriving outside in the gathering dusk he had made an educated guess about the amount of rent she would be paying for unusually spacious accommodation there. It was almost unheard of for a single person in Japan to enjoy the luxury of a flat with a spare bedroom: a three-room-diner-kitchen or "3DK" in the jargon of real estate agents commonly housed a family. Although the building lacked the latest gimmicks and the ostentatious touches of luxury offered in the newest developments at the upper end of the market, Miss Johnston was fortunate indeed; but then her living expenses were no doubt heavily subsidised by the private women's college which was her main employer.

After opening the door the few inches the safety chain permitted and satisfying herself as to her caller's identity the English girl had taken some time to release the chain, and

154

her movements were clumsy and listless as she closed the door after him and fumbled to secure it again. It was cool inside and at first Kimura found the rumbling of the air-conditioning unit set into the outer wall of the living room distracting. "It's all right," she said when she had followed him in. "As a matter of fact I did have an engagement this evening, but it was cancelled."

"I see." Kimura nodded sympathetically, aware that her lover was in the company of Junko Migishima at that moment, and wondering how often during the course of their affair Murata had stood her up. "Sit down, do." Penny gestured vaguely at the single armchair in the western-style room. "Would you like a cup of coffee? It's only instant. Or I've got some whisky. Suntory, if that's okay."

Kimura clung to austere principles in the matter of coffee and gratefully accepted the alternative, interested to see that she followed his example and that the drinks she poured from a full bottle were generous to the point of extravagance.

Penny pulled out the nearest of the four straight chairs ranged round the small dining table and sat facing him, the whisky bottle within easy reach. "Well, what can I do for you?"

"I need to ask some more questions about Marianna. I'm sorry."

"I didn't think you'd come to read the meter."

"I beg your pardon?"

Penny made a small gesture of apology. "Sorry. You speak English so well I forget to make the usual allowances. Very unprofessional of me." A sad half-smile illuminated the pale little face and Kimura could see for the first time what might have attracted Murata. At the same time he objected to being classed with her students. It offended him that she should even think of "making allowances" for inadequacies in his comprehension and command of spoken English, about which he was justifiably vain.

"I was brought up in the States and I understand you just fine, Miss Johnston. Just didn't quite catch what you said is

155

all.'' He paused to make sure the rebuke had sunk in, and then leaned forward, the very soul of sincerity. ''Believe me, I hate to have to badger you like this, but there are still aspects to this case that worry us. And I think you can help us to straighten things out.''

Penny lowered her head and shook it slowly, then looked up at him. The purplish blotches under her eyes were very noticeable and a muscle at the corner of her mouth twitched. ''What's the point? Marianna's dead. You can't do anything about that.''

''We can do something about it, even if it's not in the way you mean. And we must.'' Kimura paused for effect as he reached out, gently took the now half-empty whisky glass from her hand and placed it on the floor beside him. ''We think she was murdered, you see.''

He was ready for anything from a gasp of disbelieving horror to hysteria or a fainting fit, but quite unprepared for what in fact happened. It was as though an invisible hand caressed Penny's face, soothing the tension and anxiety away and leaving her exhausted but at peace. Kimura had on very rare occasions seen something similar happen to women immediately after orgasm and been uplifted by the experience. Now he was astonished to see Penny blink, look at him as though seeing him for the first time and then ask him politely if she could please have her drink back.

''You know, then,'' she said simply after she had emptied her glass and poured herself another, seemingly unembarrassed by the fact that Kimura's drink remained practically untouched. Kimura stared at Murata's mistress, utterly baffled. Her relief at the news that the police were treating Marianna van Wijk's death as a case of murder was as incomprehensible to him as the fact that she had obviously been planning to spend the evening in Murata's company before Junko Migishima had offered herself to him as a more intriguing prospect. He struggled to control his own expression and make some sort of response.

''We know, yes,'' he managed to say at last. ''And we have a vague sort of idea how. But why? That's where we're
156

stuck and need your help. The fact that you had . . . obviously come to the same conclusion encourages me to hope that you'll give that help.''

Abruptly Penny stood up and walked over to the window and slid a fitted *shoji* screen into place across it. The Japanese touch it provided was out of keeping with the proportions and furnishings of the room but greatly improved the look of it, not least by cutting off Kimuta's earlier view of the neighbouring block of flats, identical in externals to the one he was in. The feeling of being enclosed also in an odd way helped him to concentrate. "I can try I suppose," Penny said then. "But it would only be guesswork. The main thing is that you know he killed her. I can't tell you what a relief that is.''

Kimura tried manfully to make some sort of sense out of the situation. "Miss Johnston," he began. "When I came to see you at the university I thought you were understandably upset, but now I realise you must have been very frightened too. Why on earth didn't you confide in me then?''

"I . . . I didn't know then. That she'd been murdered. You see, I had no idea what that building was—the one where she was found. Then when I did find out I began to put two and two together, and it was absolutely terrifying.''

"Why?''

"Because . . . things began to make sense, and I had to accept that it would occur to him that I could have worked out what must have happened. And that he might decide to . . . do something like that to me as well.''

"Didn't you find it hard to accept that he was capable of such a thing? In view of . . . everything?''

"Of course I did. I still do. He's a very attractive man. Always been nice to me. That's the awful thing.''

Kimura shook his head from side to side in exasperation. "But you've kept all this to yourself, that's what I can't understand. Your friend almost certainly murdered by a ruthless killer, and then on top of that to be in fear of your own life and yet still go on . . . what are you playing at, for heaven's sake?''

157

Penny had by then completely thrown off her earlier lethargy and with a sharp gesture of the hand seemed physically to brush his words away. Her eyes were brighter and a touch of colour had come into her sallow cheeks. "Never mind that now. The important thing is that somehow or other you've found out, and I wasn't the one who put you on to him. So long as he realises that . . . have you any idea where he is now?"

Kimura looked at her in renewed surprise. "Yes. As a matter of fact I have. That is, I know *who* he's with, but it might be better if you don't—"

"Then for God's sake why don't you arrest him?"

"We shall, soon. We know most of the facts now, but getting proof is another matter. What I'd like to do is make quite sure that you're safe for the next two or three days until he's properly in the bag. Is there anywhere you could go? Some friend you could stay with, preferably away from the Osaka-Kobe area?"

"Course I got a friend, course I have. Very dear friend, but might be a bit awkward . . . got plans, you see. Wants me to keep in the background for a while. Besides, there's my teaching and . . ."

Three very large whiskies had heightened her colour and begun to make her slur her speech, but it was the dark flush which mantled her neck as she winked at him with owlish deliberation as well as what she said that at last alerted Kimura. It was all he could do to stop himself blurting out the first words that came into his head, but fortunately after falling silent Penny seemed to have retreated temporarily into a private reverie and Kimura held his tongue as he struggled to reconstruct his thoughts out of the rubble into which she had made them collapse.

How could he have been so crass? Why had it taken so long to dawn on him that Penny was talking about Shimizu, not Murata? *Did* she know something of crucial importance which implicated Otani's son-in-law beyond all question? Were they all in fact on the wrong track?

A remark Otani had made during their last telephone conversation swam unbidden to the surface of his memory. "You see, Kimura-kun, I do realise that it's difficult for me to propose solutions to this problem when I'm actually part of it." Although he tried to dismiss it from his consciousness, the idea that Otani might deliberately have misdirected his most trusted colleagues found a precarious lodgment in Kimura's mind and made him feel physically queasy. It also set him ranging desperately back over the course of the investigation and some of its odder features.

Why at first had Otani been so concerned to withhold from him knowledge of the discovery of the photograph among the Dutchwoman's possessions? Why had Otani yielded so meekly to Hara's bureaucratic insistence that he should withdraw from a case involving a member of his family? Otani was quite wily and quick-witted enough to have trumped Hara's ace by pointing out that under the law Shimizu was not in fact a member of his family; that on the contrary his daughter Akiko was now a member of Shimizu's. And why, having formally ruled himself out of the proceedings, was Otani in practice still directing them so effectively from home, sending Noguchi, Hara and himself along paths which all led in the same general direction?

Kimura roused himself, suddenly aware that Penny Johnston was staring at him glassy-eyed, a slackness about her mouth which encouraged him to hope that with any luck she had missed the implications of one or two of the things he had said before realising that they had been talking at cross-purposes. "So sorry," he said. "I was just thinking about possibilities. On second thoughts, perhaps I was being overcautious. It might be better after all for you to stick to your usual routines, especially now that you know we're closing in quickly." He felt he needed a drink himself at that point, swallowed half the remaining contents of his glass and coughed and spluttered as the alcohol caught at his throat. "Sorry again," he said when he had more or less recovered his composure, spoiling the effect by hiccuping immediately afterwards. "You were going to tell me why."

"Why?"

"Yes, why. Why he killed Marianna. In your opinion."

"Well, obvious. Obvious." Penny poured another heroic slug of whisky into each of their glasses. Kimura thought it quite likely that she would pass out before long, and for all his anxiety to hear what she had to say he doubted if he would get much sense out of her even if she did remain conscious. The point was academic, because at that moment the telephone rang and Penny made a lunge for it, knocking her chair over in the process.

"*Moshi-moshi?*" Even in the circumstances Kimura found it hard to repress a grin as he reflected that even a drunk could have no difficulty with the all-purpose Japanese telephone phrase. Penny continued in English, a happy, if lopsided, smile on her face.

"Course it's me . . . Forgive you? I shall have to think about that, after you being so horrible. Anyway, you're a rotten fibber. Bet it wasn't business at all . . . but as long as you've got rid of her . . . Lonely? Hoo! You're not the only pebble on the beach, my fine-feathered fish in the sea . . . Pissed? Course I'm not . . . Just you come over here and say that again . . . Where are you, anyway? . . . Good, *that's* not far . . . Naughty! I'm not telling. You'll have to come and see for yourself . . . Only an hour? A mingy *hour*? Oh well, better than nothing. If I know you a lot can be done in an hour . . ." She went into a fit of giggles as she put the receiver back and then assumed an expression of childish solemnity on turning to confront Kimura.

"My friend," she said unnecessarily. "Mustn't catch you here. Very jealous, my friend."

"Ah. I'll be off, then. You've been very helpful—and thank you for the drink." Kimura hurriedly got up, and himself carried his glass over to the kitchen unit in the corner and rinsed it out, doubting very much if it would occur to Penny to do so. Then something made him go to her and hold her lightly by the shoulders. "You'll be all right. I'm sure of it," he said, more to reassure himself than her. "Er, please don't mention our conversation to anyone, will you? Anyone at all."

Penny Johnston shook her head with great seriousness.

"Promise," she said. "He was so cross when I told him you came to ask about Marianna the first time." She seemed to have sobered up slightly, but to be unaware that tears were streaming down her cheeks, or that Kimura took a paper handkerchief from his pocket and dabbed them dry for her, then kissed her gently on the forehead. He released her and went to the door. "I'll be in touch," he said as he unhooked the chain. "We'll get everything sorted out soon. Take care."

Once outside the building he walked round to where he could see the window of Penny Johnston's flat. It was just after nine, not an unreasonable time for a man to call on a mistress who lived alone. Murata seemed certain to receive an ardent welcome, for Penny had so obviously been sexually excited by the mere sound of his voice on the phone. Kimura wished there were some way of checking quickly with Junko Migishima on Murata's state of mind when she left him. He hoped he had made the right decision. Penny had presumably been alone with her lover on several occasions since the murder and had come to no harm so far; and even if he was completely on the wrong track and her fear of Shimizu had some justification he could hardly harm her while he was living under discipline in a remote Zen temple in the Yoshino mountains.

All the same Kimura could not bring himself to go. He found himself a discreet observation post in the shadows, and five minutes later watched Murata get out of a taxi and go into the apartment block. He stayed much more than the "mingy hour" Penny had mentioned on the telephone, and Kimura's anxious vigil lasted until Murata left just before midnight. Then, hurrying round to the side of the building again, Kimura was much relieved to see a blurred shadow moving about in Penny's flat and, briefly, her unmistakable silhouette close behind the shoji screen. He wondered if next time they met he should hint to her with all delicacy that in that moment it had been obvious to him and presumably to any of her neighbours who happened to be looking in that direction that she was in the nude. It was small reward for a long and needless wait to set against his misgivings and uncertainty, but a pretty sight all the same. Penny Johnston might be small and skinny, but she was not without her physical charms.

Chapter 21

"**A**H! INSPECTOR KIMURA. HOW GOOD OF YOU TO JOIN us."

"Morning. I hadn't realised you'd moved into here. You've certainly made the place look different. Quite a home from home. Good morning, Junko-san."

It was a long time since Kimura had set foot in the main office of the criminal investigation section and he was struck by the transformation in its appearance. When the unlamented Inspector Sakamoto had been in charge and occupied a separate, spartanly furnished cubby-hole nearby, the place had looked like a barrack-room, the furniture lined up as if for inspection. Now the desks were set at jaunty angles, the floor was covered with hard-wearing but colourful carpet-tiles and an array of indoor plants provided a simple screen for what amounted to a reception area furnished with a low table and a set of inexpensive vinyl-covered easy-chairs.

Behind what was obviously Hara's own desk in the far corner was a cork board displaying a year planner and a number of official notices, but elsewhere art posters decorated the walls, and the whole room looked comfortable and friendly. Ninja Noguchi was already ensconced in one of the chairs, looking like a derelict who had dropped in for a nap.

"Good morning, Inspector Kimura. Welcome to Grand Hotel. That's what my husband calls it." Kimura had never heard his own assistant Migishima utter anything remotely resembling a *bon mot* and was startled to think that frivolity might enter into his relationship with the wife who outranked him. He was also impressed by the evidence of Hara's imaginative managerial style and Junko's ease in the presence of her boss, and more than a little jealous.

"I'm surprised he hasn't demanded similar luxury for the Foreign Affairs Section," he said with a touch of severity as he took the chair Hara indicated with a courtly gesture. "Well, we must get on, I suppose. A lot to be done."

"Indeed there is," Hara said. "Junko-san will of course be preparing a written report of her conversation yesterday evening with Dr Murata, but time presses and I thought it would be best if she were to give us all an informal account right away. I will just explain first the plan devised to enable her to gain his confidence."

There were times during the next few minutes when Kimura was hard put to it to remain silent and he did in fact emit one yip of outrage, only to think better of interrupting decisively when Noguchi opened one tortoise eye, glared at him in magisterial rebuke and growled, "Save it, Kimura."

Hara appeared not to notice and continued with donnish precision to describe the approach adopted with such panache by Junko in her telephone call to Murata the previous afternoon, and with something of a flourish played back the tape of their conversation. Only then did he explain in detail what was proposed for the next and decisive stage and turn to Junko. Having courteously invited her to report on her meeting with Murata, Hara sat back with an air of mingled complacency and anxiety, like a fond parent watching a child perform a party piece.

"Yes. Well, as you gathered from the tape, he didn't exactly play hard to get," Junko began. "He suggested meeting at six-thirty by that avant-garde mural in the booking hall of the Keihan Line station at Yodoyabashi in Osaka and arrived five minutes early. I'd tucked myself into a quiet corner a few minutes before that, so I was able to look him over before I

164

went up and spoke to him. He obviously thinks he's God's gift to women, and that type's always very easy to handle.''

She directed a smile of angelic innocence in Kimura's direction and continued after the briefest of pauses. "The idea of drinks had already been mentioned on the phone and he took it for granted that we were going to his favourite bar, so I hopped in a taxi with him and off we went to Dotombori. He was a perfect gentleman on the way, I may say.''

The smile had not been lost on Kimura and he listened grimly, losing the thread of Junko's story momentarily only when, to his amazement, he saw Hara reach forward to the loaded tray on the table between them and pour out four cups of coffee from a vacuum flask, place little packets of sugar and powdered cream substitute in the saucers and distribute them, *beginning with Junko*. And she let him do it, accepting her cup with a gracious little nod. It was an unheard-of breach of Japanese office etiquette, and Kimura allowed himself to wonder briefly if . . . but surely not? *Hara?* And *Junko*? He had after all called her "Junko-san" to her face in the presence of witnesses . . . Kimura gave his head a little shake and received another shock when he saw Noguchi dump the contents of the paper packet into his coffee, stir it and slurp it down with every evidence of satisfaction: Noguchi, who never drank coffee and barely touched the green tea invariably provided by Otani when he summoned his lieutenants to confer with him in his office. The times were out of joint indeed.

". . . so-called 'private club'—one of these 'bottle-keep' places, but up-market," Junko was saying when he pulled himself together. "Most of the bottles I saw were premium brands: plus several of Scotch. The one with Murata's name on a plastic tag round the neck was American bourbon, actually. Jack Daniel's Black Label.''

"Look, I don't like to interrupt, but I don't really see the relevance of all this," Kimura said. Junko Migishima sipped her coffee and looked at him with composure.

"It's relevant, Inspector. The tag was a new one. It confirmed the strong impression I received from the kind of fuss the mama-san made of him when we arrived that he hadn't been a so-called 'member' very long. I can imagine that Dejima Pharmaceuticals pay him pretty well as director of research, but even so he was acting as if he had money to burn. And he was . . . how can I put it, expansive. He said right away that he agreed to do the television interview, and said in effect that the president of his company could like it or lump it, because he didn't expect to be staying with Dejima very long anyway. At that stage I couldn't get him to say what he planned to do, so I extracted his life story from him instead.''

''And was *that* relevant?'' Kimura was becoming more and more restive as Junko continued to dominate the proceedings, with Hara and even Noguchi seemingly hanging upon her words. She remained unruffled.

''Only insofar as it made him relaxed and so impressed by the sound of his own voice that he began to be convinced I was easy game. In fact he *has* done pretty well. His father's a carpenter in some little town in Shikoku, mother was a maid in the local inn till she took off with the assistant cook there when Murata was eight. After that he had to fend pretty much for himself. He had side jobs of one sort and another all through middle and high school but stuck to his books too and sailed through the Kobe University entrance exams. From then on it seems he was the golden boy, except for a year or so when he got carried away during the campus troubles and ran around with some of the most extreme radical activists. But the professor of pharmacology talked him back into the fold and took Murata on as his research assistant right after graduation. Then he won a Fulbright scholarship to the United States for two years, a doctorate at twenty-seven and a series of research jobs in the pharmaceuticals industry before he was head-hunted by the Dejima president and helped the new company get off the ground. Even making big allowances for his inflated ego I think he really did do most of the work of developing Gynojoy, and that's what has really made Dejima's reputation in the past year or two.''

''So he is still a working scientist, then?'' Hara asked.

''Oh yes, very much so. I suggested that his job as director of research and development must involve a lot of burden-

166

some paperwork but he said he refused absolutely to concern himself with such things.''

"Just to follow up this point a moment, did he indicate that he was engaged on any particular research project at the moment?''

Junko nibbled at her lower lip with very white little teeth. "Not in as many words, but even given that he's a man who obviously goes through life well pleased with himself he did hint more than once that Gynojoy was by no means his only achievement . . . and that he'd be doing Fumio Iwai a favour by condescending to appear on the programme.'' She giggled, obviously enjoying the undivided attention of three senior officers. *"Mankind's Modest Benfactors* is a laugh, I must say. Perhaps it was a mistake on my part to have given him quite such a come-on when I spoke on the phone, but after a few drinks he turned the conversation to the subject of aphrodisiacs and smiled rather smugly when I asked if he'd done any research in that field. He asked me whether I hadn't noticed an 'interesting side-effect', as he called it, of taking Gynojoy regularly. I don't know if you've noticed the advertising for it, gentlemen, but it has what you might call overtones.''

Kimura snorted. "Absolute rubbish! I've seen some of those ads. They just play on women's suggestibility. Everybody knows a new drug can't be marketed without passing the most stringent government tests, especially for general sale without prescription. This Gynojoy stuff is probably mainly aspirin and vitamin B6 if the truth be known . . . anyway, can we please come to the point? Did he or didn't he let anything slip to suggest that he might be synthesising stimulant drugs for illicit distribution? It seems to me we're on very shaky ground indeed here, setting up what amounts to an entrapment with only a wild hypothesis to justify it—''

"I'm sure you're right to be cautious, Inspector.'' It was Hara, calmly judicious. "And I think nobody here seriously expects Murata to convict himself out of his own mouth on television. Or indeed actually to appear on television. We do however hope to obtain a revealing video recording later today, and if all goes according to plan this might constitute valuable corroborative evidence. The fact that Dr Murata is a conceited person is encouraging. Given the right environment and incentive he will find it hard to resist the temptation to boast about his work, and there seems little doubt from what we have heard that Junko-san has predisposed him to be indiscreet.''

''Give you any trouble later, did he?'' The force of Noguchi's personality was such that no matter how long he remained silent it was never possible to forget he was in a room. All the same, all the others reacted with a start when he spoke with unusual vehemence, and for the first time Junko looked slightly embarrassed. Both Hara and Kimura awaited her reply with some trepidation, knowing that Noguchi had acted as go-between at the Migishimas' wedding and that he took his continuing responsibility for their marital welfare very seriously.

''No. Nothing I couldn't handle,'' she said carefully, her cheeky urchin face going bright pink. ''I had been leading him on, after all, and I didn't want to make him angry enough to refuse the interview. So when he suggested that I might like to show my gratitude for the benefits of Gynojoy in a practical way I didn't say I was married or turn him down outright. I . . . er, I let him think I fancied him but that it would have to be a pleasure deferred because it was an awkward time of the month. He was, well, a bit upset to say the least but I teased him and said he could hardly be short of girlfriends and that surely one of them would be glad to wind up the evening with him . . . and it seemed to work. 'Well, in the circumstances perhaps I *will* just make a quick telephone call,' he said in a very sophisticated way. And he did just that, or pretended to. He might have been just saving face, of course, but he came back obviously ready to leave and we parted quite amicably.''

Hara looked towards Noguchi who seemed to be in a state of deep gloom but said nothing, and then nodded sagely. ''Excellent,'' he said, glancing at his watch. ''And now we really should be off.'' Kimura made no attempt to get up as Hara and Junko stood. ''I don't like it,'' he said. ''And I'm saying here and now that my opinion will go on record in my report. But I can't stop you, I suppose. Mind if I have a word with you, Ninja?'' Noguchi too remained firmly in place as Kimura turned to him ostentatiously in mute dismissal of the other two.

Hara coughed deprecatingly. ''Do by all means remain here as long as you wish, gentlemen,'' he said. ''Well. I shall let you know as soon as possible how things transpire.''

The door had barely closed behind them when Kimura gave vent to his accumulated spleen and anxiety. ''Ninja! I just don't understand you! When I think of the times you've shot me down when you thought I was sticking my neck out . . . and now you don't lift a finger to stop Hara going through with this crazy half-baked scheme! And involving Junko-san like that, too. Though I've got to admit that she seemed willing enough to play the prick-teaser . . . she even embarrassed *me* once or twice with all that talk about—''

''Shut up.'' Noguchi spoke more quietly than he had to Junko, but his eyes were blazing and the words stopped Kimura dead in mid-sentence.

''I'm sorry, Ninja,'' he said after a lengthy pause. ''But I'm seriously worried.''

''So am I,'' Noguchi said. ''All right. What's on your mind?''

Chapter 22

"**H**E'S ASLEEP ALREADY," OTANI SAID AFTER HE HAD TIP-toed down the stairs of the western-style house in Senri New Town which was not much smaller than their own home but in comparison meanly proportioned and poky because of its small windows, unyielding interior walls and obtrusive furniture. "Pity, but I suppose it's just as well really. It's pretty late after all."

He had gone to the Shimizu home directly from the Kin-tetsu Line's Osaka terminus and before anything else gone upstairs, looking forward to settling his mind with one of the courteous little conversations with his grandson which in happier times Hanae found so comical, even though Otani pointed out to her rather stiffly that some of Kazuo's ideas about the world were a great deal more sensible than a lot of what you heard on the television.

Hanae and Akiko were sitting in the living room talking quietly together and looked at him without apparent interest. It was as though mother and daughter had instinctively erected a wall of feminine solidarity between themselves and him, and since neither offered any comment he went through to the kitchen and opened one of the cans of chilled Kirin beer he had picked up near the local station and brought with him to the house.

"That's a revolting habit, Father," Akiko said as he came back, swigging directly from the can. "There are plenty of glasses in the kitchen." Both women knew of his visit to the temple and his meeting with Akira Shimizu there, for he had spoken to Hanae from the payphone outside the rural station before setting out on the return journey, told her briefly what had happened and learned from her that Akiko had returned to Senri with Kazuo immediately after Hanae's own shopping expedition with him. It was Hanae who had urged that he should ring Akiko at once with the news and suggested they should all meet there so that he could fill in the details and Hanae could be on hand to offer any support that might be called for. Otani had no doubt that Hanae and Akiko had talked at length since then both over the phone and at the house before his own arrival there.

He ignored his daughter's rebuke and took another thoughtful pull at the beer in the silence that followed. Hanae gave him a half-smile and went into the kitchen herself, returning with a plate on which was a plump roll of savoury cold rice stuffed with lengths of raw tuna, cucumber and pickled radish and enclosed in a sheet of pressed seaweed. "You must be hungry," she said. "I bought you a *futamaki* on the way here. It's been in the fridge so it should be nice and cold."

"Oh. That was nice of you. Thank you." Otani had eaten nothing since breakfast and though once or twice during the long round trip the thought of food had broken through his preoccupations he hadn't felt hungry enough to do anything about it. Now he did, and began to dispose of the *futamaki* in short order. "I did tell you he sent his love, didn't I?" he said between mouthfuls.

Akiko closed her eyes and breathed heavily. "Men," was all she said, but there was a world of bitterness in her voice.

Otani eyed her warily, and she intercepted the look when she opened her eyes again. They were wide with anger, but her voice was icily controlled. "He sends his love, does he?

171

How very kind of him. And like a typical male chauvinist you sit there stuffing yourself and drinking beer and calmly pass on the message as though it was a postcard from somebody on holiday—''

''Aki-chan.'' Hanae spoke quietly, but with great effect. ''Your father is hot, hungry and thirsty, and very tired. However upset you are you shouldn't speak to him like that.''

Otani managed something resembling a smile. ''It's all right, I probably deserved it. It was tactless of me to come out with it like that. He hasn't telephoned you yet, then?'' Akiko shook her head slowly, her eyes brimming with tears until she ripped a paper handkerchief from an open box beside the television set and scrubbed them dry.

''I'm sure he will later this evening,'' her father went on. ''Probably waiting to be sure young Kazuo's settled. I was quite surprised to find there's a phone at the temple, in Aoki-*sensei*'s private quarters. Of course, Akira hasn't had access to it during the past week but I'm sure Aoki won't raise any objection now. Or he could walk down to the station and use the public telephone there. He told me he has money.''

''He could just as easily come home, couldn't he?''

''Could he?'' Otani looked at his daughter with mingled tenderness and concern. ''He doesn't know that yet, of course. Always assuming you mean it. And then again it's not for me to speculate about whether he wants to. I can only say that he's been through at least as traumatic a time as you have, my dear, if not worse. In any case, for safety's sake he must stay where he is for another couple of days. Just until we make the arrest.''

All the time he was speaking Otani watched Akiko's face. He saw uncertainty there, and something like hope fighting to dislodge the cold, settled anger which had returned to her eyes. It was something, if not much, and he permitted himself to think that, in spite of the new complications it had revealed, his mission had at least enabled him to chip at the foundations of Akiko's despair. The food and drink had

172

helped to revive his own spirits, but Hanae had been right. He was tired, and he wanted to go home.

It was as though Akiko read his mind. "You *are* confident about that?" she asked. "Making an arrest soon?"

Otani licked his fingertips, sticky from the rice, and nodded. "Yes. It can't be long now."

"I see. Well, in the meantime I've got some thinking to do. I'm sorry I was rude to you, Father. But it's been a difficult time."

"I know. Thank you for what you told me this morning. It was a great help when I met Aoki at last."

"If you say so. Look, Mother, thank you for coming over. Both of you. But would you mind leaving me alone now? You must both be tired, anyway."

Hanae was tempted to suggest that they should be wildly extravagant and go home by taxi, but once outside in the street Otani seemed to brighten up a little, so she held her peace and they set off in the direction of the station. He stopped short after a few paces.

"Listen! Isn't that the phone ringing back in the house?"

"I'm not sure. I can't hear anything now, but it might have been," Hanae said, more to please him than because she really thought she had heard anything. "It's a little cooler, don't you think?"

There were a few breaks in the clouds and the evening air, though still very warm, was soft and velvety rather than soupy and oppressive as it had been before dark. Otani grunted in what Hanae interpreted as agreement, but seemed disinclined for conversation and they walked on in a silence which was companionable enough. Hanae never minded biding her time, and during the subway ride into central Osaka and the rest of the journey by commuter train to Rokko she confined herself to asking about his journey and the precise location and appearance of the Zen monastery where Akira Shimizu had taken such unlikely refuge. Otani said he had been told that not counting their son-in-law there were five monks under Aoki's tutelage but that he had seen only two of them at a distance and spoken to neither. After so many years he

173

could not possibly have said whether or not they were also former radical activists.

It was Otani who turned the subject to Akiko's state of mind and the prospects for the future of the Shimizu marriage, and the two of them speculated fruitlessly until they reached home and Otani thankfully let them in. It seemed an eternity since he had set out late that morning after his conversation with Akiko, and after washing all over and then immersing himself chin-deep in the square bathtub, in water much less hot than he usually liked, he almost fell asleep.

Hanae roused him, not by saying anything but by simply being there so that he suddenly became aware of her presence in the doorway of the little bathroom. "Feeling better?" she asked when he sat up and removed the damp, skimpy little towel he had made into a pad and balanced on his forehead.

"Mm. Ready for bed, though."

Hanae had already changed into a cotton yukata, and sat on a cork-topped stool out of splash range. "I had a bath before I went to Senri," she said. "I wonder if Akira's rung her yet?"

"Ah. So do I. Hope so."

"It would help me to understand," Hanae began carefully, "if you would tell me why it is necessary for Akira to stay in that place until somebody is arrested. If you know he had nothing to do with that poor woman's death, then I don't see—" She stopped and drew back the hem of her yukata as Otani hauled himself to his feet in a cascade of water, a good deal of which slopped to the tiled floor but ran safely away down the central drain.

"Perhaps I am being over-cautious," he said, rubbing himself down with the wet towel and wringing it out vigorously from time to time. "But in any case as I tried to hint to Aki-chan, he didn't say in as many words that he wants to leave. Don't forget the main reason he went to Aoki in the first place. It was to sort out his feelings about the foreign woman—and about Akiko too, I imagine."

He reached for the folded yukata Hanae was holding on

her lap and she handed it over as it was rather than opening it out and helping him on with it as she usually did.

"And what about Akiko's feelings about him, may I ask? Don't they enter into it?"

Otani looked at her in puzzlement as he tied his narrow sash, then reached out a hand and pulled Hanae gently to her feet. "Well, of course they do," he said. "But that isn't what I was talking about at that precise moment. It isn't like you to be so illogical. Shall I make some green tea?"

It was the one thing he could do quite well in the culinary line, and within a few minutes they were both sitting at the plastic-topped table with the little tea-kettle between them. Otani had found a packet of rice crackers in the cupboard and tipped them on to a plate, and he crunched a few pensively before reopening the conversation.

"I'm sorry you seem to be accusing me of male chauvinism too," he said eventually. "All I meant was that Akira was overcome with guilt. Has been, ever since Marianna van Wijk got in touch with him again here and they resumed the affair they'd been having in London. Guilty about being unfaithful to Akiko, presumably, and wondering what to do about the situation. He really loved the other woman, I think, which would have made things that much worse. I expect that's why even before all this happened he was moody and difficult and they've been going through a bad patch. That and the practical problems of readjusting after living so lavishly in England."

Hanae nodded agreement, surprised at his acceptance that the Shimizus might have been less than delighted to return to Japan.

"Then on top of everything else the death of Marianna van Wijk, for which Akira was in no way responsible but for which rightly or wrongly he blamed himself. Aoki-*sensei*— it's funny you know, Ha-chan, but even with what I know about his past I can only think of him as the Zen master he is now . . ."

"He seems to have impressed you," Hanae said, unobtrusively topping up his cup.

"Yes, he did. He has an extraordinary personality. I can

175

quite see why Akira made use of him as an occasional confidant over the years since they stopped being politically active. You know, until today I've always found it impossible to see the point of all those stories about famous Zen masters bullying and striking their disciples. Couldn't imagine why anyone in his right mind would voluntarily submit to being insulted and brutalised like that. I still can't conceive of subjecting myself to anything of the kind, even if I were a lot younger.''

"Nor can I," Hanae said.

"What? Oh. Have you got any more of these crackers? Oh, good, I'll finish these up then. Anyway, as I say, the death of his woman friend must have shattered Akira, and what he knew or imagined he knew about its circumstances frightened him. He's still finding it hard to credit the conclusions he came to . . . that's why he didn't point the finger earlier, and even Aoki had a hard time getting him to open up to me. He's been too confused to realise that behaving as he has would inevitably make him a suspect, much less that he might be at risk himself. Anyway, Aoki was the only person he could think of to turn to, and Aoki decided to deal with first things first. Don't ask me how his brand of therapy worked, but somehow or other he pulled Akira to pieces emotionally and made it possible for him to start putting them together again for himself.''

"But . . . but darling, aren't you forgetting something?''

"Probably. What?''

"Akira disappeared *before* that day. The day the Dutch girl was killed. So he couldn't have been in that critical state of mind when he went to the monastery, could he?''

"I wish you hadn't asked me that, but yes, he could. Because Aoki-*sensei* told me that he didn't turn up there until Sunday evening. And that he was in great distress when he did.''

Hanae gazed at her husband wide-eyed. "Then what—''

Otani slid his hand across the table and held hers. "What had he been doing in the previous twenty-four hours or so? I'm sorry, I can't tell you that. Not before I've found out for sure myself.''

176

Hanae abruptly pulled her hand away and put it to her mouth, her eyes wider than ever. "Darling, you aren't . . . you aren't *shielding* Akira, are you? Even for the sake of Akiko and Kazuo, you wouldn't . . . surely not anything like . . . ?"

"Of course not," Otani said shortly. "Don't be ridiculous."

Chapter 23

"**A**RE YOU QUITE COMFORTABLE THERE? SUN NOT IN your eyes? All set, everybody? Good, let's make a start, shall we? Hold the camera till I give the word." Inspector Takeshi Hara referred briefly to the papers attached to the clipboard on his knee. Then he dabbed at his broad forehead with a paper handkerchief, glanced at the neat little microphones clipped to the two participants' shirts and looked up again to beam encouragingly at the Dejima Pharmaceutical Company's director of research.

When it came to the point, Dr Murata had thought of a number of reasons why it would not be such a good idea for the rehearsal of his interview with Fumio Iwai to take place against a background of elaborate chemical apparatus in the laboratories of Dejima Pharmaceuticals, and Hara was on balance relieved when it was finally agreed that the run-through would be in the car park, with the logo on the facade of the company buildings in shot throughout. He had complete confidence in the skills of the taciturn police technician in jeans and sweatshirt operating the video camera and thought the bogus Kansai Television stickers on his equipment were quite good enough to pass muster so far as the little knot of casual onlookers who had appeared from nowhere were concerned. In any case, they were soon shooed away by two Dejima Pharmaceuticals security men who then retired to a discreet distance at a haughty sign from Murata.

Junko Migishima gave Hara no cause for anxiety. With stopwatch in hand, sunglasses buried in her hair high above her forehead, her own clipboard and a giant felt-tip marker pen suspended from a ribbon round her neck she looked the perfect media person in tight white trousers under a bright blue shirt tailored like a man's, the tail hanging free over her compact little bottom. Certainly her manner with Murata struck Hara as being exactly right, and it was obvious from the heavily charged, meaning looks they were exchanging from time to time that the scientist bore Junko no personal grudge over having been kept at arm's length when he last met her and entertained lively expectations of better luck next time.

What had mainly bothered Hara from the first was serious doubt about his own ability to sustain the role of a television producer with any conviction, and the idea of doing it in the open air instead of in a corner of a laboratory within sight and earshot of other researchers who might be presumed to be intelligent, sophisticated people was comforting. He was in any case gaining confidence with every minute that passed with Murata exhibiting no sign of suspicion and Fumio Iwai himself having been affable and helpful from the moment he arrived at the wheel of his own sporty Mazda car.

"I've been looking forward to meeting you," Iwai was saying to Murata. Like Hara, both men were seated in plastic chairs brought out from the office building. "Nearly didn't make it for this run-through, though. I'm supposed to be up in Hokkaido filming. My team have been looking into the situation of the Ainu aboriginal people there for one of my *I Accuse* programmes. Ah, well, it'll keep. We'll play it more or less by ear today and I'll look through the video first thing tomorrow. Of course we'll have a warm-up together on the day right before the show, so as to discuss any supplementaries and put you completely at ease."

"I'm not in the least nervous about it, Mr Iwai, I can assure you," Murata said, twisting the heavy signet ring he wore on the little finger of his left hand round and round. "In fact, I wonder if these . . . ah, preliminaries are really necessary. However . . . By the way, I may have a copy of this video myself in due course, I take it?"

Hara intervened. "That goes without saying, Dr Murata. Sayoko! Make a note to strike another copy, please!"

"As good as done." Junko directed a dazzling smile impartially among the three men, impressed by Hara's airy command of the jargon they had both been studying so recently and the fact that he had remembered to use her *nom de guerre*. She thought that so far he was doing a good job of suppressing his normal pedantic manner, coming across as an intelligent, rather earnest and basically shy man who might well make a successful career in television behind rather than in front of the cameras. It would have been awful to have tried to carry the thing off in the company of Fancy Pants alias Kimura, whom she could, unjustly, imagine turning up for the occasion wearing riding breeches and a celluloid eyeshade and brandishing a megaphone.

"Right, gentlemen," Hara continued. "As Fumio knows, we're planning for this chat to run about eight minutes, in two parts on either side of a commercial break—"

"I should like to have details of the commercials it is proposed to show."

This time it was Junko who chipped in. "Well now, Doctor, even Fumio himself doesn't have any control over that, I'm afraid, and neither does Takeshi here, but one of them's certain to be for Gynojoy. I'll do my best to find out and let you know."

"Yes, do that, Sayoko," Hara said tightly, shocked to the depths of his being by Junko's audacious and wholly unnecessary use of his given name. "Time's getting on. If you're ready, Fumio? Dr Murata?"

"Yes. This has already taken longer than I had expected. I have to budget my time very carefully, you know." Fumio Iwai rubbed his mouth to conceal a grin and then nodded gravely at Hara, who blinked apologetically at Murata.

"I'm sorry. We do realise you're a very busy man. But I think we're all set now. Okay, quiet please everybody."

Hara gestured to the cameraman, who nodded acknowledgment and shifted his battery-belt into a more comfortable position. Then he swung his lightweight equipment to his shoulder and switched it on, directing it at Junko who now brandished a clapper-board. "August thirteenth. *Mankind's Modest Benefactors*—Naotaka Murata. First sequence, Take One," she announced in a smooth, professional way, and then unobtrusively withdrew as the camera took in the company logo in the background and then focussed on Murata and Iwai.

"Well now, Murata-*sensei*! Welcome to the show!" Iwai began with the air of genial malice which characterised his interviewing style. "The applause you just received from the studio audience tells me we were right on the button in asking you here today to take a bow as the first of *Mankind's Modest Benefactors* to appear in this series. But tell me, shouldn't it be *womankind's* benefactor?"

"Well, of course I'm flattered to be thought of as any kind of benefactor, but it's quite true that my research has been directed to making life a little easier for the ladies—"

"At those very tricky times that they don't like to talk about. And millions all over Japan are grateful to you."

"I'm honoured if that's true."

"Our mailbag tells us it's true. And if by some remote chance any of our viewers—our *lady* viewers—haven't guessed yet what it is I'm discussing with this wizard of the test-tube, it's a miraculous product called Gynojoy. Yes, this little bottle I'm holding up contains a secret formula which literally changes a girl's outlook on life, not once but thirteen times a year. How long has it been on the market, *sensei*?"

"A little over eighteen months."

"You mean you discovered it so recently?"

"No, no. Of course not. Besides, it's not accurate to talk about one man *discovering* a pharmaceutical product. It never was, even in the case of penicillin. I suppose I would have to agree that novel applications for some substances—like penicillin—occurring in nature have been stumbled upon or dreamed up by an act of imagination, but pharmaceutical researchers nowadays tend to start with an idea of the effect

181

they'd like to produce and then *create* something to give the idea reality. And they mostly work in teams. Gynojoy owes its existence to the dedicated efforts of a lot of people, not just to me.''

"Of course, and I'm sure the good people in the studio audience would like to give your associates a big hand . . . Thank you, thank you. All the same, *sensei*, let credit be given where credit's due, and we know who leads the team. Tell me, what gave you the idea of trying to tackle the problem of premenstrual tension?''

"When I was doing graduate research in the United States I was associated with a project to improve the standard birth control pill—''

"Which isn't legal in this country is it?''

"No. No, it isn't.''

"Is that on account of the side effects?''

"It's not for me to say. All I can tell you is that it hasn't been approved by the government drug registration authority . . . but for what it's worth, the project I mentioned *was* concerned with the elimination of certain side-effects and, ah . . . perceived risks in using the pill over a long period of years. And it occurred to me that it might be possible to sort out the regularly recurring hormonal imbalances which almost certainly trigger off PMT in a great many women—''

"And so the idea of Gynojoy was born! Fantastic, Doctor. Stay with us, everyone, because I'll be talking to Dr Naotaka Murata again right after these messages. OK, cut.'' Iwai looked towards the cameraman and raised his voice a little. "I'll do that announcement again direct to camera after we've finished, along with the noddies,'' he said, then sat back with a casual wave of the hand to Hara while the cameraman wound back the tape and began to check its quality in his viewfinder.

"That was fine! Really great!'' Hara enthused. "You're a TV natural, Dr Murata.''

"I should still have preferred a preliminary sight of the questions.''

"What, and lose this marvellous spontaneity? Anyway, don't forget, this *is* your preliminary sight of the questions.

182

We just have to make sure you give your answers as much zip and zing on air. Want a Coke or anything, either of you? Or shall we go on?"

"Okay by me," Iwai said. "You ready, *sensei*?"

"Oh, very well. But look, I hope you won't be pursuing this business of the birth control pill. It isn't approved for prescription in Japan but it might be one day and meantime there's no bar on research. All the same it's not something that ought to be discussed at a superficial level."

"Not to worry. I hadn't planned to raise the subject. I was just responding to what you said yourself. Right, let's get the other half on tape, shall we?"

Hara glanced towards the cameraman again

"Was the take OK?"

"Yup. All checked."

"Good. Let's go, then. Sayoko?"

Junko consulted her stopwatch and made a note before repeating her performance with the clapper-board, and the "Second sequence, Take One" began.

"Hello again, viewers! And for the sake of those who may have just joined us, let me explain that I'm talking today to pharmacologist Naotaka Murata, the first of a remarkable group of people we on the *Fumio Iwai Looks Sideways* show are calling *Mankind's Modest Benefactors*—retiring geniuses who have in various ways transformed the lives of millions. And the *sensei* has just been telling us how he hit on the idea which resulted in Gynojoy, the product which enables women all over Japan to say goodbye to premenstrual tension woes! Did you have any trouble getting your wonder-drug approved for general sale, Doctor?"

"No. No, we didn't. It was subjected to extensive testing and clinical trials of course, and met every requirement of the national pharmaceutical authority."

"So, no side-effects, then?"

"No adverse side-effects whatsoever."

"Ah-ha! No *adverse* side-effects? How about *nice* side-effects? It can't come as a surprise to you if I mention what an awful lot of our viewers already know . . . that not to beat about the bush, the word is that Gynojoy makes ladies feel

183

sexy. After all, your advertisements don't exactly deny it, do they?"

"I'm just a scientist. I have nothing to do with marketing or advertising my company's products. And I can't really comment on the rumours you mention . . . except to say that if women begin to feel good at a time of the month they normally associate with depression, tension and soreness in the breasts, well, it wouldn't be surprising if they enjoy a more active and pleasurable love life as a result, would it?"

"Whatever you say, Doctor. Anyway, all the evidence we have suggests they do, and you'd better prepare yourself for fan mail by the sackful now that our lady viewers have seen you in the flesh! Now before you hurry back to your lab, let me just go back to what you said a while ago about creating a drug to have a particular effect. Here in Japan, of course, we have very strict stimulant drug control laws, but people still risk severe penalties to smuggle the stuff in because of the money to be made out of selling amphetamines and so forth."

"Well, yes . . . but I—"

"Now in the United States there are people cutting out the necessity for smuggling by making what they call 'designer' drugs—compounds which have the same effects as the main illicit drugs, or even greatly enhanced effects. And for a while at least these designer drugs weren't even illegal. Now, you're in the business of altering people's states of mind—"

"Now wait a minute!"

"You just said as much, *sensei*. Quite legally, of course, and in the process making countless women grateful to you, not to mention the shareholders of the Dejima Pharmaceutical Company. There's no law against euphoria that I know of. Or making people feel sexy. Ever been tempted to create an aphrodisiac pure and simple, Doctor?"

"Of course not! It would be completely unethical."

"Lots of fun, though. Just for the sake of argument, could you?"

"I—well, it is theoretically possible, I suppose, but quite out of the question."

"I'm not sure I follow you there, but let it pass for a

moment. Of course, if he *weren't* quite so scrupulous, a man with your scientific knowledge and creative imagination could make a fortune that way. I mean, when you consider the vast sums spent in Asia alone on things like rhinoceros horn and musk—''

''Look here, I am not prepared to continue the discussion along these lines!''

''Oh, really? Pity. It was just getting interesting. I'm a little puzzled that you seem so embarrassed—''

''Just what are you insinuating?''

Junko Migishima crossed her fingers, hoping that Murata was becoming angry and confused enough to forget the whirring of the video camera.

''Not a thing, *sensei*,'' Iwai continued blandly. ''We're here to honour you, not try to trip you up. I just thought that since you said earlier that there's no bar on *researching* unapproved substances you might . . . Oh well, never mind. Let's change the subject before we sign off, shall we?'' He took a deep breath and stared bleakly at Murata. ''What exactly is your relationship with the gangster Ikuo Motoyama?''

Murata gaped at Iwai for a moment in silence, his face drained of colour. Then his eyes opened very wide, he closed his mouth and looked round wildly. Seeming to become aware of the proximity of the cameraman at last he launched himself out of his chair, sending it clattering to the asphalt surface of the car park and attacked the technician, almost succeeding in grabbing the camera before Junko Migishima was there and Murata yelped as one of his arms was expertly twisted up behind his back. The technician phlegmatically went on filming as Hara spoke.

''My colleagues and I are police officers, Dr Murata, and I have to inform you that I have reason to believe that you are a material witness in the case of a citizen of the Netherlands, now deceased. You are therefore required to accompany me to prefectural police headquarters for questioning.''

''I'm going to let you go now, *sensei*,'' Junko added quietly. ''And if you'll take my advice, calm down and come quietly. It may be too late anyway, because there's someone

185

at one of the upstairs windows and that funny little receptionist is watching us like a hawk from inside the main entrance. But they may not have seen your little outburst, and you don't want it all over the company, now do you?''

Otani waited with the other casual onlookers until he saw Hara and Junko drive away with Murata in one unmarked car and the technician load his gear into another while apparently sharing a joke with Fumio Iwai. Then, when Iwai strolled over to his own car, Otani moved away unobtrusively and headed back towards the nearest bus stop. He was lost in thought when the Mazda pulled up beside him.

"Get in," Iwai said through the opened window. "And take off those horrible plastic sunglasses. You look like a cheap tout, but don't imagine I didn't recognise you. The least you could have done is come over and ask for my autograph.''

Chapter 24

STILL ANXIOUS AND UNEASY, KIMURA HAD JUST ARRIVED at the main entrance on his way out of the building when through the glass panels of the big swing doors he saw the familiar figure of Otani's driver Tomita bustling up the steps outside. He stopped in his tracks, because this could mean only one thing; something reassuring but at the same time hard to account for. His thoughts in turmoil, Kimura watched Tomita haul one heavy door open and hold it in position, standing respectfully to attention. Kimura could now see Otani below, exchanging what looked like a friendly word or two with the policeman in the blue coveralls and visored helmet of standard riot control gear on duty outside. Then Otani turned away and mounted the steps himself, nodding his thanks to Tomita as he reentered his domain after almost a week's absence. He was looking dapper in summer uniform and his swarthy face lit up with pleasure when he saw Kimura standing there; and for all his doubts and misgivings Kimura found it impossible not to respond.

"Morning, sir. Welcome back," he said, briskly correct for the benefit of the old former patrolman who presided over the visitors' book inside the entrance hall and was a stickler

187

for the formalities. Otani resumed his habitual expression of dispassionate gravity and saluted politely: being as always in plain clothes Kimura could only bow his head in acknowledgment.

"Good morning, Inspector. Good to see you. Good morning, Takahashi-san. On your way out, Inspector?"

"I was, sir, but it isn't an urgent matter."

"Good. If you could spare me a few minutes in my office before you go I should be grateful. And I don't suppose Inspector Noguchi's free, by any chance? Or Inspector Hara?"

"I'm not sure, sir. I'll check right away."

"Thank you. I'd like five minutes in any case to look through whatever's landed on my desk while I've been away."

Otani's face was now completely unreadable, and without waiting for Kimura to reply he started up the main staircase towards his office. Kimura watched him out of sight and then went back to his own ground-floor room where he collected his increasingly bulky folder of notes on the van Wijk case. He thought it very likely that Noguchi was still with Hara in the open-plan criminal investigation section where the three of them had been talking together a few minutes earlier, and he was right. When he re-entered the room Noguchi was sitting back in one of the inadequate black vinyl visitors' chairs with his feet on the low table, while Hara had brought a straight chair to his side and was sitting on it crouched forward so as to bring their heads within a few inches of each other. One or two of Hara's staff glanced up incuriously from their desks as Kimura passed, but the two inspectors were too absorbed in their confidential conversation to notice him until he stood over them like a figure of doom.

"Sorry to interrupt the summit conference," he said sourly as Hara looked up in surprise. "He's back. Breezed in just as I was going out of the building and wants to see us all in five minutes.

At this even Noguchi turned his head and peered up at Kimura. "How does he seem?"

"Seem? Perfectly normal, might never have been away. In uniform. Well, how are we going to play it, Ninja?"

Noguchi made a growling sound which might have indicated amusement. "Since when have we ever played anything with him? Except his game?"

Hara looked from one to the other of his more seasoned colleagues and coughed. "If I may say so, gentlemen, I do think that before we report to the superintendent it would be helpful to know whether there have been any telephone or other contacts between him and any of us in, say, the last twenty-four hours. I . . . well, I feel a little embarrassed to admit that he telephoned me at home late yesterday evening and asked me to give him a brief account of the interview with Murata. I understand that he had already been in touch with Fumio Iwai, which is hardly surprising. The superintendent did ask me to regard his call as confidential but even so I realise now that in the circumstances I should have told you both about this when we first met this morning. He said nothing to me about returning to duty today."

Noguchi showed no reaction to the news, and Kimura guessed that this was probably what Hara and he had been talking about when he came back into the room. "Better late than never, I suppose," he said. "I haven't been in touch with him since he rang to tell me he'd found Shimizu. What about you, Ninja?"

"Had a word or two with him on the phone last night."

"What about?"

"This and that. Motoyama mostly."

"Did he tell you he was planning to come in this morning?"

"No. Better go up and find out why he has."

As Noguchi dealt with the lengthy business of getting to his feet Hara went over to his desk and returned with his own file of notes. The three men then headed for the door in instinctive order of seniority with Noguchi at the head of the procession, Kimura next and Hara bringing up the rear.

Otani's door was open and he must have heard their approach because he was on his feet to greet them as they filed into the familiar office and waved them at once to their accustomed chairs. "Good morning, Ninja! And there you are, Hara, good. Well done, Kimura-kun, a full house. How nice to see a bit of blue sky, isn't it? Makes the air feel much less muggy." The old tin tray with the cups and kettle of green tea was in place and Kimura found himself cheering up for no particular reason except that things seemed somehow right again after being at sixes and sevens for much too long. Otani was obviously in no mood to be hurried, and chatted on about the weather while he distributed tea all round. Then he took an appreciative slurp at his own cup, put it down and settled back, eyes bright as he looked at each of his principal lieutenants in turn.

"Gentlemen. I'm very pleased indeed to see you all together again, and grateful to you for sparing the time when I realise you must all have other pressing matters to attend to. So I'll try to be brief. First, as you will have gathered, I have returned to duty as of this morning, on the instructions of the chairman of the prefectural public safety commission who telephoned me at home late yesterday afternoon. It seems that the district prosecutor wishes to interview me."

In the lengthy silence that followed Noguchi stirred slightly. "He's been kept in the picture," he said at last.

"I'm sure he has, Ninja. Copies of all written reports sent to his office, at least one comprehensive briefing from you during my absence on duly authorised leave, everything strictly in accordance with the rules. No problem there. No, I said he wants to *interview* me, in the belief that I may be in possession of information of a personal nature relevant to his investigation of the murder of Marianna van Wijk. In short, not as commander of this force but as Tetsuo Otani, father-in-law of one of the principal suspects. Nevertheless, the chairman considers it desirable that I should not remain on leave, and I understand that the prosecutor has no objection to my coming back to work."

"And are you, sir? In possession of information, I mean?"

It was Hara who spoke, earning himself a glare from No-guchi as he did so. Otani looked at him expressionlessly.

"Yes, I think I probably am, Hara. But then all of us are, aren't we? And like me, you've no doubt been making hypotheses on the basis of that information, and so has the prosecutor unless I'm very much mistaken. The question is, which of several hypotheses can be sustained, isn't it? Anyway, I've no doubt that Mr Prosecutor Akamatsu will have a good deal to say about the propriety or otherwise of my actions when I call on him, so I hardly think it necessary to debate that particular issue here." He looked at his wristwatch. "My appointment is for just over an hour from now, so we must get down to business, gentlemen. I should like from each of you a brief—very brief—statement of your own understanding of this case and your opinion about where we should go from here."

He looked again at each of the others in turn, his expression now clouded with what looked to Kimura like pain. "I want you to be completely frank with me and each other. You . . . one or other of you might feel inhibited or embarrassed about speaking your mind, out of a conflict of loyalties perhaps. In case that is so, it might help if before we begin I tell you that my own wife suspects that I might have been shielding my son-in-law from the consequences of his actions by attempting to pervert the course of justice. I should not be surprised to hear of similar misgivings on the part of any of you and hope that no one will hesitate to give voice to them if they are present in his mind. Inspector Hara, will you begin, please? I won't interrupt."

Long afterwards Otani often referred to Hara's exposition as a model of its kind. Although his folder of notes was open on his knees he did not refer to it once during the following six minutes or so, and paradoxically, in view of the tension raised by Otani's own introductory remarks, he spoke with none of his usual deprecating hesitation. There was still a touch of pedantry in his manner and choice of words, but the way in which he marshalled his ideas and related them to the circumstances in which Marianna van Wijk's body was found, her links with Akira Shimizu and through him and her friend Penny Johnston with Naotaka Murata was masterly. He covered the background to the burning down of the Hinomaru Building and the relationship between Murata and the gangster Motoyama with clarity and economy, accounted neatly for Shimizu's retreat into hiding and then offered his reasons for identifying Murata as the murderer. Only when he had finished did he take off his glasses and indulge in a prolonged bout of blinking while he polished them.

"Thank you, Inspector," Otani said. "I envy you the orderliness of your mind and your apparently total recall of the salient features of this complex and puzzling affair. Beyond admitting that I am somewhat relieved to infer that you don't think I've interfered for disreputable motives with the course of the investigation I'll reserve comment for the moment if you don't mind. Kimura, would you share your thoughts with us now, please?"

Kimura took a long time to respond to the invitation and then kept his head lowered and spoke so quietly that Otani leant forward in his chair, obviously straining to hear; but it was Noguchi who interrupted by growling "Speak up!" Kimura looked up in confusion and began again.

"I'm sorry," he said with transparent sincerity. "Truly sorry, but I don't agree with Hara. I very much wish I did. Murata is a conceited, stupid and reckless man . . . and you've often enough pointed out to me that I ought to know a thing or two about people like that, Chief." It wasn't much of a joke but it did momentarily lighten the atmosphere, even though Otani felt more like weeping than laughing, moved by Kimura's gallantry.

"I mean it," Kimura went on. "He's all those things, but I don't see him as a murderer. He's a criminal, certainly. I don't doubt that he's been conning Motoyama and other gangsters with a lot of big talk about supplying designer drugs. Might even have run up a few samples; might indeed be seriously planning to go into production. I've seen the videotape of that interview and my own feeling is that he probably is trying to synthesise a true aphrodisiac. I know

192

he hasn't admitted anything yet but he'll crumble soon enough under questioning. In view of what we already know I can believe he was in on Motoyama's scheme to raise the money he was demanding—possibly suggested it. I rule him out of the role of murderer, though. And I certainly can't see why a *yakuza* boss like Motoyama should want Marianna dead. So I'm forced to home in on Shimizu." Otani could see the pleading in the intelligent black eyes fixed on his face, but merely nodded and after a moment Kimura continued.

"I'm sorry, Chief. But I can't shake off the fear that you haven't been completely candid with me, at least. You asked the others to delay telling me about that photograph. I don't know why. Nor do I know exactly what you may have said in your various phone conversations with Ninja here or Hara." Otani noticed that Kimura's hands were shaking, took a packet of Hi-Lite cigarettes out of his tunic pocket and wordlessly offered it to him. Kimura took one with a nod of acknowledgment, lit it with the lighter he always carried although he hardly ever smoked and dragged hungrily at it. Sighing out a great blue-grey cloud of smoke he passed a hand wearily over his forehead and then spoke again.

"I can't possibly improve on Hara's summary of such facts as we all know about. In particular, I'm not overlooking the apparently damning evidence of the old lady near the Hinomaru Building who identified Murata running away; but we all know that won't really stand up without corroboration. Shimizu and Murata are much of an age and build, and it would have been simplicity itself for your son-in-law to fix himself up with a false moustache and fluff his hair up to give himself a passing resemblance. And I can think of reasons why he might do that precisely so as to divert suspicion to Murata: *staging* the running away as conspicuously as possible in the hope of being spotted." He sucked again at the cigarette and blew out another cloud of smoke before continuing.

"But consider Shimizu's motivation. Marianna had turned up in Japan and resumed a relationship he thought belonged

193

to his London days and had ended there. But once they met again he couldn't resist her, even though guilt feelings were putting a strain on his marriage and indirectly affecting his performance at work—and it's obvious he's an ambitious man. They start sleeping together again and he gets into more and more of an emotional tangle, until Marianna precipitates a crisis by telling him she's pregnant. He transfers his guilt to her, blames her, comes to see her as the focus of all his problems. He's at his wits' end when through her English friend he meets Murata, an obnoxious and temperamentally very indiscreet man he knew in his student days to be none too principled when it came to taking care of his personal interests. Shimizu—perhaps even with Marianna's help—puts two and two together and figures out roughly what Murata is up to with Motoyama. It offers him a way out of his predicament: he decides to kill Marianna and finger Murata for the crime, perhaps even convincing himself that by putting Murata out of circulation he'd be doing society a favour. And he does bring himself to kill Marianna, perhaps by strangling, after getting her to meet him at the Hinomaru Building.''

Kimura broke off and looked at each of the other men in turn. ''There's a big question mark here, obviously. How did he know the place would be deserted that day? We shall have to ask him, but I suppose Murata could have let something slip. Anyway, whatever the explanation the thing is done, and only afterwards does it hit him. Result, breakdown. Complete mental collapse and he runs to Aoki, his old mentor, for protection and—what? Punishment perhaps, who knows? What we do know is that he didn't turn up at the temple where you found him until the day after his mistress died. That's all I can contribute.''

Kimura sank back, his face pale and drawn. Otani turned to Noguchi, who for once had both eyes wide open and focussed on him. ''It's a powerful indictment, Ninja,'' he said quietly. ''Which of them do you think did it, Murata or Shimizu?''

''You're giving us a hard time, Commander,'' Noguchi said, the everyday coarseness of his speech replaced to shocking effect by a careful formality. "You've given us a tough week, too. I'm impressed by what Kimura just said, and by his guts in saying it, and I don't mind telling you that there've been moments when I thought he was on the right lines. But I've had another talk with Motoyama and I go along with Hara. Murata had a motive. He was so pleased with himself he told his girlfriend what he was up to. She told the Dutch girl and he found out. Maybe this Marianna was shocked and threatened to spill everything she'd discovered to the Dejima personnel guy, Kano, the one Kimura talked to. I don't know. What I do know is what I said to you on the phone last night: that it's time you stopped messing us about. This isn't some sort of parlour game and we deserve better from you. If you are covering for Shimizu I can understand it, but in that case you've blown it by coming back here today. If you're not, stop fucking about and tell us your own ideas straight."

During the electrifying silence which followed them the hurt anger of Noguchi's final words was answered by the blazing fury in Otani's eyes as he put his hands on the arms of his chair and made as if to rise. Then he lowered himself again, his body relaxing and his expression changing.

"I . . . I accept your rebuke, Ninja," he said at last, his voice thick with emotion. "With difficulty, and in the special circumstances because I owe my apologies to all of you, not least Kimura-kun." He paused, breathed heavily and rubbed his eyes. Then he hesitated before turning to Hara. "Is there any tea left in that kettle? No? Oh well, never mind." He drained the bitter dregs in his cup, pulled a face and sat back. When he next spoke it was more calmly.

"It was in my judgment necessary for me to ask the three of you to work independently on various aspects of this case during the past week or so. Only thus could I hope that you would turn up the evidence I hoped you would find to support what was at first little more than a mere feeling on my part. But I gravely mishandled the earlier part of this meeting, gentlemen, and I'm sorry. The fact is, I have not been shielding my son-in-law because he did not kill Marianna

195

van Wijk. I will tell you who I think did, and why. Then, always assuming I can persuade you I'm right, I'll explain what I've arranged with Akira Shimizu and what I'd like you to do while I go and try to make my peace with the district prosecutor . . .''

Chapter 25

AKIRA SHIMIZU HUNG BACK AS THE OTHER PASSENGERS getting out at Rokko streamed through the ticket barrier. The sound of their automatic umbrellas mushrooming up to ward off the warm rain which greeted them outside was clearly audible to him and it was a relief when the orderly commotion at the station entrance died down and he was able to slip quietly out. Taxis had been in brisk demand a minute or two earlier and there were none waiting, but even as he peered up at the bruised, slate-grey sky one splashed into the forecourt and stopped with a flourish in front of him. The rear door swung open invitingly as the driver operated the remote-control lever but Shimizu shook his head, pulled up the collar of his jacket and set out on foot.

It had been not much more than a week since he had last been dressed in a suit, but it felt completely alien, and not only because he had lost weight and it flapped round his limbs strangely as he laboured up the hill. He felt like an actor in costume and was in fact unconsciously mumbling his lines, arousing the curiosity of passers-by who peeped from the sheltering gloom of their umbrellas at the eccentric ''salaryman'' talking to himself, apparently unaware of the fact that his hair was already plastered to his forehead by the rain which had darkened his shoulders and trouser-legs.

Shimizu had wept as he left the temple early that morning, and looked back longingly at the dull sheen of its roof tiles when he reached the wayside shrine before which his father-in-law had stood in brief meditation on his way to find him. He had been barely conscious of sitting in the train, changing to the subway at the terminus in Osaka and then again to the Osaka-Kobe commuter line he knew so well. From time to time he had tried to empty his mind in the way Aoki had taught him, and somewhere behind everything lay the awareness of that blessed space and stillness which he had once or twice glimpsed even in the depths of his self-hatred, bewilderment and despair. That morning, though, it seemed that nothing had changed and nothing could be changed. Thoughts of what had passed and what lay ahead of him jangled and jostled in his head and he was exhausted, frightened and dizzy with uncertainty. He had dreaded the prospect of obeying Otani by making the crucial telephone call from Aoki's quarters. In the event he had somehow found the strength and mental agility to handle the conversation. The arrangements he proposed for the rendezvous were not only accepted at once but with seeming approval. Shimizu told himself that what he now had to do was equally demanding but perhaps just a little less difficult. For he would not be in charge.

He rounded the corner into the familiar street and approached the old wooden house with the two Chinese characters for ''Otani'' deeply incised one above the other into an oblong slab of wood mounted vertically on the gatepost, near the little metal token showing that the occupants had paid their national television licence fee. The front door rattled open as Shimizu entered the outer gate.

''Come in, come in,'' said Inspector Jiro Kimura. ''You're in good time, but you''re absolutely soaked, man. We can't do much about your trousers, but get your shoes off and I'll try and find a towel for your hair.''

* * *

"Good of you to come, Superintendent," the district prosecutor said with little warmth, taking in the resplendence of Otani's best uniform.

"You summoned me, Mr Prosecutor."

"Yes. Yes, with great reluctance. I am so sorry to have interrupted your well-earned leave. Do please sit down, Superintendent."

"Thank you. It's of no real consequence. I didn't go away anywhere. There are always things to be done at home, I find, but when the chairman of the public safety commission said you wanted to see me I thought I might as well get back into harness as from today."

"You've been at home all the time, then?"

"Yes. Well, out and about locally, of course, and I spent a few hours wandering round the Yoshino hills one day. It's still quite unspoiled there once you get off the beaten track, I'm glad to say."

Otani watched Akamatsu fiddle with his letter-opener, a rather fine ivory specimen but nothing like as impressive, Otani thought, as the miniature samurai sword on his own desk. "You've kept in touch no doubt with your colleagues about the van Wijk case?"

"They were bringing me up to date in the office this morning before I left to come here," Otani said, and the letter-opener clattered to the polished surface of his desk as the prosecutor dropped it, clenched his fists and sat back in exasperation.

"Please. Credit me with a modicum of intelligence. It's perfectly clear to me that you have been giving the orders throughout in this investigation, and that important information has been withheld from me, presumably at your instigation."

"That's a very grave charge, Mr Prosecutor."

"I am well aware of the fact. At the moment, however, it remains in the air between us, as it were. But before we go further I have to say that I am fully prepared and indeed expect to lodge a formal complaint to the National Police Agency about the impropriety of your conduct and your reluctance to collaborate with me."

"That is of course your privilege, Mr Prosecutor. Though I confess that I find it difficult to follow your train of thought. Inspector Noguchi assures me that progress reports have been submitted to your office daily and that he has himself called on you to brief you."

"Otani-san. Look, I don't want to quarrel with you—"

"Oh. I was under the impression that you did."

"Damn it, hear me out! I have questions to ask you. I am fully entitled to ask them and you are under obligation to reply. Is that much agreed?"

"Of course."

Akamatsu exhaled noisily and relaxed his posture. "Good. Then let us proceed on that understanding. What have you in fact been doing during the past few days?"

"Helping my daughter to find her husband. He went missing." Otani's face was expressionless.

"You are referring to Akira Shimizu?"

"Yes."

"Why was I not informed?"

"My daughter and her husband live in Osaka Prefecture. Quite apart from that, my daughter decided against reporting the matter to the authorities. That is her right, of course. So I made a few purely personal enquiries in my private capacity."

"But you knew very well that Akira Shimizu was acquainted with Marianna van Wijk."

"No."

"What do you mean, no? You must have done."

"No, sir. It is true that I suspected that my son-in-law had known her, but that is a long way from knowing it. I did not find out definitely until he told me so himself."

"I am a lawyer, Superintendent, and I should like you to know that your careful selection of words does not impress me. You do however now admit that you found Shimizu?"

"Yes. He was in a religious retreat. Undertaking a course of Zen discipline. It's not at all uncommon for business executives to do something of the kind these days."

"That is so. Such executives usually do so with the knowledge and approval of their employers, though. Whereas you have already acknowledged that Shimizu disappeared from his home and went into hiding. This was a highly significant and suspicious thing for him to do, was it not?"

"I had comparatively little difficulty in tracking him down."

"In your purely personal capacity, of course. That does not surprise me. Well, Otani-san, since even you now accept that Shimizu is a material witness in the van Wijk case it should come as no surprise to *you* to learn that I wish to question him myself. Where is he now?"

Otani looked at his watch. "So far as I know, he's at my own house in Rokko. My wife has gone to spend the day with our daughter and grandson in Senri New Town. I expect my son-in-law will join them there later, but he wanted to have an important conversation in private with somebody first and my house seemed a good place for it."

Otani braced himself for an explosion, but Akamatsu shook his head slowly as he stared down at his desk. Then he looked up in what looked to Otani like simple dismay. "I'm sorry, Otani-san. Sorry that a man of your distinction should apparently have taken leave of your senses. How can I possibly overlook the fact that you have allowed a prime suspect in a murder case to do what he likes, meet whom he likes . . . in your own house?"

"Oh, it's all right," Otani said. "Inspector Kimura and Senior Woman Detective Migishima are there too, you see. Out of sight, of course. Because the person my son-in-law is probably talking to by now murdered Marianna van Wijk."

By the time he heard a taxi pull up outside and the doorbell finally rang Akira Shimizu had dried out to some extent though his trousers were still clammy. His hair was combed and a cup of coffee with plenty of sugar had helped him to concentrate his mind in preparation for his forthcoming ordeal. He was in shirt-sleeves, the sodden jacket of his suit on a hanger behind the door of the kitchen where Kimura sat in silence with Junko Migishima. Shimizu went to the front door and slid it open.

"Hello. You found your way, then."

"Yes. The directions you gave me were quite clear. The Otanis are your parents-in-law, are they?"

"Yes. But they're both out. Won't be back till this evening. Come in. I'll take your umbrella."

The rain had eased off but it was still drizzling outside, and Shimizu knocked most of the water off the umbrella before propping it carefully in a corner of the stone-floored entrance hall.

Penny Johnston slipped out of her high-heeled shoes and stepped up on to the tatami matting as Shimizu indicated the way to the living room.

Chapter 26

"NO, HARA WASN'T IN THE LEAST OFFENDED. IT HAD to be Kimura, you see, because the conversation was in English. He said Akira speaks it extremely well, even though he must have been under great strain all the time. And obviously Junko-san had to be here when the arrest was made."

Hanae clasped her hands and pressed her lips together worriedly as Otani spoke. She had not been back home very long and kept looking round the room anxiously, as though fearful that the dramatic events which had taken place there in the morning must have left physical traces. Otani himself looked quite relaxed, wearing a yukata and sprawled in his favourite corner opposite the television set. Only the unaccustomed sight of a glass of whisky and water at his side signalled to Hanae that he was more on edge than he pretended.

"She really did try to kill him with an ice-pick? But you said she's so tiny."

"Yes, she is. And of course Akira was expecting to be attacked and the others were nearby so he was in no real danger, even though he did turn round only just in time and got that nasty wound on his hand. Better that than a stab in the back, but just as well they gave him an anti-tetanus shot at the clinic. An ice-pick can be a deadly weapon even for a little creature like Penny Johnston if the victim's back is turned. The Dutch woman was twice her size but totally unsuspecting, of course. Penny Johnston killed her from behind and said so in as many words when she was struggling with Akira. Junko-san wanted to intervene at once but Kimura held her back until enough had been said to leave no possible doubt about what had happened that day at the Hinomaru Building and why. Are you interested?''

"Am I *interested*?' Hanae's voice rose to a squeak and Otani's mouth twitched as he reached for his drink.

"Yes, of course you are. Well, to put it as simply as possible, Penny Johnston is besotted with Murata and was determined to marry him. She's an intelligent woman and realised that he was venturing into dangerous waters by concocting these designer drugs I was telling you about and offering to supply them for distribution through the *yakuza* network, but when she tried to talk him out of it he bewitched her with the prospect of making a fortune quickly and then slipping out of the country to go to America where he promised to marry her. It's conceivable that the two of them might have managed it, too, if Marianna hadn't appeared on the scene.'' He swallowed the remaining contents of the glass and began to get up to go and get another drink, but Hanae took the glass from him.

"You stay there. I'll do it,'' she said, and hurried into the kitchen.

Otani called after her. "You say Kazuo-chan was asleep when Akira got there?'' he called after her.

"Yes. Just as well,'' Hanae said through the open kitchen door. "I left, of course, as soon as Akira rang from the station to ask Aki-chan if he could come home. The poor girl only had ten minutes to get ready for him and needed that time to herself.''

"What did she say to him? When he asked if he could go home?''

"What I expected,'' Hanae said, returning with his refilled glass on a tray with the Scotch bottle, a jug of water and a bowl of ice cubes. On the tray there was also an opened

204

half-bottle of domestic rosé wine, misted from the refrigerator, and a glass for herself.

"She said, 'I suppose so, you stupid idiot,' put the phone down and burst into tears." She handed him his drink and poured a glass of the wine.

"Do you think—"

"We can only hope so, leave them alone and wait and see. Go on about poor Marianna."

Otani shook his head in disbelief. Now that Penny Johnston and Naotaka Murata were both in custody his main concern was what might be happening at the Shimizu home, and he found Hanae's matter-of-fact attitude to it faintly shocking. "Yes, I suppose you're right," he muttered, then shook his head briskly and carried on.

"Marianna soon sized up the situation between her friend and Murata, and during her time at Dejima Pharmaceuticals hit it off very well with the personnel man Kano who invited her home to meet his wife. Kano had been keeping an eye on Murata himself. He's a religious man, and sensitive with it, according to Kimura. Somehow he must have communicated to Marianna his uneasiness about what Murata might be up to. Marianna tried to find out more about Murata from Penny Johnston, who jumped to the conclusion that Marianna was attracted to him. No doubt Murata himself added to her jealous fears when he met Marianna at her flat. It seems he's something of a ladies' man and we know that Marianna was a very striking-looking woman." He stretched and yawned.

"There are still a great many points to cover when we get down to questioning them properly, but so far as I've been able to work out at this stage Marianna confided in Akira who had in any case met the *yakuza* boss Motoyama. Akira probably tried to talk her out of it, but she was obviously a bold, impulsive sort of girl, and she decided to go and have a look at the Hinomaru Building. Which, of course, before it was burned down looked quite impressive; so much so that she marched straight in on some pretext or other and no doubt had a good look round before they got rid of her. If it hadn't ended so tragically one could almost smile at the thought of a bunch of thick-headed yakuza trying to cope with this formidable foreign woman claiming to be doing research into Japanese business methods. Motoyama must have been horrified when he found out. Meantime Murata knew about Motoyama's plan to raise the money he was demanding by setting fire to his own headquarters building, and also that it would be empty on that Sunday. Unfortunately he told Penny, who was by this time determined to kill Marianna. She therefore told Marianna that Murata wanted to see her urgently at the Hinomaru Building and got in herself—through the garage probably. When Marianna arrived Penny let her in and killed her, hoping that her body would be too badly burned in the fire for any wounds to show. And for a time she was lucky, because it did work out like that. The old lady Hara and Junko Migishima interviewed probably did see Murata. No doubt he went along just out of curiosity to see if the place really would go up in flames, then thought better of it and pushed off in a hurry. It's most unlikely that he knows his girlfriend killed Marianna.''

''And where *was* Akira all this time?''

''Akira? Oh, he had been with Marianna on the Saturday and begun to be very suspicious about Murata's intentions, so he stayed away from home and then set off on the Sunday to Kashihara Shrine. He expected to find Murata with Motoyama and his hoodlums there and planned—I don't know, to confront him I suppose. And when he got back he discovered what had happened and simply fell to pieces.''

''What I don't understand is how you came to suspect the English girl in the first place,'' Hanae said, after an overlarge mouthful of wine which made her cough and splutter.

''It was my friend Fumio Iwai who gave me the idea, actually,'' Otani said. ''We were in a coffee bar and he said it was often the quiet ones who turn to murder. I never did believe Akira was capable of it, of course, but nor could I work out why on earth his foreign lady friend was mixed up with gangsters. So I looked for a quiet one . . . and when Kimura told me that Penny Johnston was trying to divert suspicion from her lover Murata to Akira I saw that there was more than one way of accounting for her behaviour.

Aoki-*sensei* followed my reasoning and between us we got Akira to fill in some of the blanks.''

He sighed. "There are still far too many left, though. And the district prosecutor's after my head unless I can persuade him I had no option but to go about things as I did. It's going to be a busy few days.''

"What will happen to her—to both of them?''

Otani shrugged. "I think she''s unhinged, myself. More in need of psychiatric treatment than prison. I expect the prosecutor will recommend she should be deported and that a confidential report should be sent through the British Embassy to the authorities in her own country. Murata will probably go to jail for conspiracy at the very least, but a lot will depend on how much of the truth we can extract from Motoyama and him between them. No. No more for me, thanks. I'm tired. Let's go to bed.''

Postlude

THE SHRILLING OF THE TELEPHONE ROUSED OTANI AND HE shook his head to bring himself back to the present as he picked up the receiver.

"Who? Senior Superintendent Nitta from the NPA? Yes, of course, put him through at once. Hello? Nitta-san! Good to hear your voice. Yes, it duly arrived. Not much chance of it getting lost on the way, more's the pity. And thanks for your note. Nice of you to write. Me? No, no special plans; I can be available any time next week. Would you like us to book you a hotel room? Oh, really? I had no idea you had a sister in these parts. Well, let me know if you change your mind. Of course. I'm sure my friend Fumio Iwai would enjoy meeting you too.

"No, as I said, nothing special, except that my wife and I are going over to Awaji Island this coming weekend with my daughter and her husband to look at a piece of land they're thinking of buying there. Grandson too, of course, he wouldn't miss a trip like that. Yes, believe it or not, they are. Tomatoes. *Tomatoes*. Never mind, I'll explain when I see you. Yes, of course it'll be ready. I haven't been a bureaucrat all these years without discovering you have to get the paperwork right. Thank you, I'll tell her. I'm sure she'd want me to give you her best wishes too. Till next week, then. Right. What? Of course I'll watch my back with you around. And I'll warn the others. Sayonara."

Otani put the phone down, took a deep breath and reached again for the draft report. Time to think about Awaji Island later, and savour the bitter-sweet memories which the prospect of returning after so many years had triggered off for both him and Hanae.

Things were very different now: the young Inspector Tetsuo Otani of those days never had to cope with a full-blown internal National Police Agency investigation of his activities. For all Nitta's joviality on the telephone it was clear that the commander of the Hyogo prefectural police force was going to need his wits about him the following week; and be able to justify every word of this wretched report.

He picked up his pen and began to amend the draft, one neat character following another with gradually increasing fluency, and was soon working on the second page.

About the Author

JAMES MELVILLE was born in London in 1931 and educated in North London. He read philosophy at Birkbeck College before being conscripted into the RAF, then took up school-teaching and adult education. Most of his subsequent career has been spent overseas in cultural diplomacy and educational development, and it was in this capacity that he came to know, love, and write about Japan and the Japanese. He lives in Herefordshire, England, with his wife and two sons, and continues to write more novels in the Superintendent Otani series.